COP 27

J. M ✓ ✓ COP 27

Whitney
MYSTERY OF THE
ANGRY IDOL

MAY 7 70 TEHACHAPI		
APR 2 6 '74 MARICOPA		
JUN 9 76 ISABELLA		
JUL 09 1991 KRV		

MYSTERY
of the ANGRY IDOL

MYSTERY
of the ANGRY IDOL

by
PHYLLIS A. WHITNEY

Illustrated by
AL FIORENTINO

THE WESTMINSTER PRESS
Philadelphia

LIBRARY OF CONGRESS CATALOG CARD NO. 65-16498

PUBLISHED BY THE WESTMINSTER PRESS ®
PHILADELPHIA, PENNSYLVANIA

PRINTED IN THE UNITED STATES OF AMERICA

To Mary B. Carver
who encouraged me to write when I
was a freshman in her English class in
Alamo Heights High School, San Antonio, Texas

With gratitude and affection

CONTENTS

1 THE WATCHER

IT HAD STORMED most of the night, and along the river, maple trees still dripped with a light patter. In the morning sun, raindrops glistened on the leaves like bright, glass beads, and the very puddles in the road had a golden sheen. Yet in spite of the rain-jeweled world and a cool summer morning, Janice Pendleton felt that she must be the loneliest girl in the whole countryside.

She stood on the porch steps of her grandmother's house and looked out over the shining width of the Mystic River, blinking her eyes against tears that wanted to come. Far above, a jet plane flew over and the sound reminded her of another plane that had taken off only yesterday for Okinawa, carrying her father, her mother, and young twin brothers. Not that she had seen them off. Before their plane had left California, her family had put her in the stewardess' care aboard another jet for the trip to New York and Connecticut. Gran had driven to New Haven to pick her up, and the two of them had come home late yesterday to Mystic.

She wouldn't cry. She would not cry! She thrust the fingers of both hands into her short brown hair, combing it furiously upward so that the tugging would hurt even more than the pain inside her.

Dad was going to stay a few days in Okinawa in order to get Mother and the twins settled. Then he would be off to Vietnam, where he was to act as a civilian technical advis for a year or more — depending on how long his special knowledge was needed. Since Saigon was not a safe or quiet place at the moment, he did not want his family there. But Okinawa was not far away and he would be able to see them now and then. Only Janice had been left behind in order to continue school in the States. She was to stay here with a grandmother she scarcely knew, and a great-grandmother she did not know at all.

That is, she would be able to stay if all went well and if her presence did not prove too disturbing to two old ladies, whose child-raising days were long in the past.

"I'm sure everything will be fine," Mother had said, "if you'll just stay away from those wild ideas that land you in trouble."

"She'll have to stay out of trouble if she wants to remain in Mystic!" That was Dad.

Otherwise, if Gran decided that having her here was too upsetting or difficult, Jan was to be sent away to school in Boston in the fall. Whether or not she would like staying here with two old ladies, Jan couldn't tell. At least they were her family. In Boston she would really be alone.

Homesickness was an ache that choked her throat and stung her eyes, misting them with tears. She had never been away from home before, and a longing for the loved and familiar was heavy within her. Last night her great-grandmother had not even wanted to meet her. Dad had told Janice what an interesting and unusual person the old lady had been in her younger days. He had told about old Mrs. Pendleton's collection of things from the Orient, and about one special piece — a strange old Chinese image that had some sort of mystery about it. But none of this interested Jan now. Especially since Gran had made it clear that almost everything upset the old lady these days and all she wanted was to retreat from the world and not let it intrude. Thus it might be some time before she was willing to have Janice come upstairs to meet her.

This morning after breakfast Gran had suggested cheerily that Jan run outdoors and explore a bit. Gran seemed to understand how she felt, but Jan had turned quickly away from the sympathy in her eyes. Sympathy would make her cry and she did not want to start that again. She had tried very hard to understand that this move had to be. But somehow nothing really helped.

She could remember the loving touch of Mom's arms about her at the airport and the wetness of tears as her mother's cheek pressed against her own. Mom had said, "Sometimes we have to cry, no matter how brave we're trying to be." Jan had done enough of that yesterday, however. Crying didn't help and tears made her feel a little sick when there were too many of them.

Blinking hard, she walked down the steps and across the road to where a grassy bank dipped toward the river. It was warmer in the sunshine and she yawned widely. She had not slept very well last night on the cot Mrs. Marshall, Gran's housekeeper, had set up for her in the living room. There had been so much thunder and lightning, and everything had seemed so strange.

She was not even to have her own room. The extra bedroom was upstairs, and that was where Great-grandmother Althea Pendleton stayed — that very old lady, only a few years away from ninety. Apparently she was still able to be up and around and to take care of herself, but she no longer came downstairs. Meals were brought up to her and Mrs. Marshall managed the dusting and cleaning in her upstairs rooms. Mrs. Pendleton was far removed from active life and not at all interested in a great-granddaughter of twelve.

Anyway, it wasn't the company of so remote an ancestor that Jan needed now. She wanted to find a friend her own age to fill the void a little. Someone to share fun and secrets with. She tried not to think of her best friend Dorothy back in Berkeley. She missed Dorothy almost as much as she missed her family. They were going to write to each other—but letters could never take the place of a nearby friend.

Down near the water where a small dock thrust outward from the rocky edge of the bank, movement caught her eye. A fair-haired boy in navy shorts and a white shirt walked out upon the dock and sat down at the far end. His back was to the shore, his legs dangling toward the water. Jan watched him for a while, but he did nothing except sit there, kicking his feet above the water. At least her interest was caught. Here was someone near her own age. The first young person she had seen since her arrival. Perhaps she could go down there and talk to him.

Her sneakers slid a bit on wet grass as she went down the bank and she landed on the gray wooden planks of the dock with a thud that made the boy look around at her.

"Hi!" Jan said, and gave him a wide, if uncertain smile.

He did not reply at once, but turned upon her the brightest blue gaze she had ever seen, looking her up and

down so critically that she could not tell if he disapproved of her yellow cotton dress and still spotless white sneakers, or perhaps objected to the tilt of her nose or the general look of her face. Something seemed to be wrong. But before she could decide that she was unwelcome and go back to the house, he spoke to her.

"Hello. Where did you spring from? I've been in this crummy place three weeks and I haven't seen you before."

"I got here late yesterday," Jan said. "I'm Janice Pendleton."

Something changed in the boy's face and he looked more interested. "You mean you're staying at that spooky house up there with the tower on it?"

Jan knew about the tower. "My great-grandfather was a sea captain," she said. "That's what they call a widow's walk. People liked to watch the ships come in back in the days when Mystic was a famous seaport. What do you mean—the house is spooky?"

The boy shrugged. "Oh, lights going on in the middle of the night. An old lady who doesn't like kids and stares out of the upstairs windows. And other things. I'm Neil Kent. We've moved into the house next door."

"The old lady must be my great-grandmother," Jan said. "I haven't met her yet, but my father says she used to be the most interesting person he has ever known in his whole life. When he was young he used to come here sometimes in the summer to stay at her house. He always liked it here." In a way she was talking to reassure herself, repeating her father's words to make herself believe in them.

Neil returned to studying the water. "Well, your dad can have it! I could have spent this summer with my cousins on Long Island. But Dad had to get this real estate thing going here, and he wanted Mom and me to come along with him. So here we are — stuck in little old Mystic, Connecticut."

"*Mystic, Connecticut,*" Jan was still trying to reassure herself as she said the name softly aloud. Because of her father's stories this had seemed a fascinating place to her ever since she was little. But it made a difference when she had to come here as a stranger, with her father and mother far away. Out on the river a motorboat was chugging by, and she looked past it toward the small white buildings on the opposite shore, the wharves where white ships were tied up, their masts and spars lifting into the sky. Beyond rose the hills that followed the river. That was Mystic Seaport over there — an old-fashioned village that had been re-created with old buildings and shops that had been moved here.

"Have you been across?" she asked Neil.

Again he shrugged. "Sure I have. Lots of times. What else is there to do around here? It's all history and tourist stuff. You can have it."

He seemed a very discouraged sort of boy, Jan thought. He had not smiled once since she had spoken to him and he seemed determined to be unhappy. In a way they were both in similar positions — not wanting to be where they were. But her own approach was a different one. She wanted to find some interest in her surroundings as quickly as possible so that the homesickness would stop hurting and she would have something new to think about.

"Tell me what else is spooky about the Pendleton house," she urged.

Neil swung around on the dock, cross-legged, and

faced her. "Was anything stolen from upstairs in that house last night?"

Jan stared back at him. "Goodness, I don't think so!"

"You didn't hear anything funny—or see anybody?"

"The storm kept me awake part of the time, but I didn't hear anything except thunder, or see anything except lightning. Whatever do you mean?"

Neil's focus of vision shifted and he seemed to be looking past her at something up on the bank. So intense was his stare that Jan was about to turn to see what had caught his attention, when he spoke to her softly under his breath.

"Don't turn around now. First find something to give you an excuse, and then have a look up there and tell me what you see."

Rather elaborately Jan moved her right foot this way and that, as if there might be a stone in her sneaker. Then she sat down on the dock facing the shore and pretended great interest in taking off her shoe. When she held it up to tap out the make-believe pebble, she took a good look up the bank. A man stood on the road above watching them. He was tall and rather thin, with short-cropped black hair and the beginnings of a beard. He looked fairly young and he seemed to be regarding the two on the dock with intent interest.

"What do you see?" Neil asked under his breath.

What was there to see? Jan put on her shoe as she answered. "Just a man up there on the road. He's a young man, I think. Sort of thin and dark and tall. I guess he's growing a beard—his face looks a bit bushy around the chin. Isn't that what you see?"

Neil nodded emphatically. His own interest had come to life and when his face brightened he was quite good-looking.

"I wanted to make sure I wasn't making things up," he said. "Dad thinks I spend half my time seeing things that aren't there. But that's because I don't care about real estate and all that stuff he feels is important. So I see other things. I think that's the fellow who was on the outside stairs of your house last night."

"Outside stairs?" Jan repeated, feeling a little foolish because until now she really hadn't been outdoors in the daylight where she could examine the Pendleton house. She looked up at it thoughtfully, and the bearded young man moved on along the road, realizing, perhaps, that he had attracted their attention.

The big white house was rather odd in its architecture. It had been built in two wings that met in a right angle. The wing that reached toward the river had a downstairs porch with wide steps across its front. The other wing ran parallel to the river, and here outside stairs mounted to a second porch and what was probably the front door of the upper apartment where old Mrs. Pendleton lived. Each wing had its own peaked roof, and at the joining angle rose the lookout tower.

"The rain woke me up last night," Neil said. "I remembered that I'd left my new bike outdoors and I came down to get it into the basement. That's when I saw a man on the stairs outside your house. He had on a yellow oilskin raincoat and a fisherman's hat pulled over his head. He was carrying something in his arms and he seemed to be in an awful hurry, as though he didn't want anyone to see him. So I stayed to watch. Just as he came down, a gust of wind blew off his hat, and the streetlight on the road showed him up when he ran after it. That's why I'm pretty sure it's the same fellow. I don't know if he saw me or not and I didn't want to hang around getting wet, so I got my bike in and went back to bed. But I wondered if you'd had a burglary over there last night."

"I don't think so," Jan repeated. The whole thing sounded very queer. Especially that her elderly great-grandmother, who didn't want to see anyone, should have had such a visitor late at night in a storm. "Could you make out what he was carrying?" she asked.

Neil shook his head. "It was something sort of bulky and dark. Maybe it was the Chinese treasure."

This boy was full of surprises. "Chinese treasure! Whatever are you talking about?"

For the first time he actually smiled at her and Jan might have felt encouraged about making friends, except that the smile was one of mockery.

"Hey!" he said. "You're old Mrs. Pendleton's great-granddaughter and you don't even know about the Chinese treasure? Mom heard about it over in town — that the old lady has a collection of valuable things from China, where she lived as a girl."

Jan knew about this, though she had never heard anyone use the word "treasure" about her great-grandmother's collection of jade objects before. Her father had been interested in these things as a boy and had told Jan about them.

"That's not a treasure," she said. "It's true that my great-grandmother was born in China in the time long before the Communists came in. Her father was Gillespie Osborn. He was a famous merchant who used to import Chinese things to the United States. He was killed in China during some kind of uprising. My great-grandmother was in Shanghai at the time and barely escaped with her life. I've heard the story often from my father."

The mockery was gone from Neil's face and he was listening with a curious intentness, a certain speculation, as if he was turning something over in his mind. At least he wasn't bored and listless anymore.

"Maybe she would do," he said, as if to himself. "Or maybe she wouldn't—being as old as she is. Probably she wouldn't make much sense to talk to."

Before Jan could ask once more what he meant, the sound of a motorboat out on the river caught Neil's attention. He swung around to look toward a small dinghy with outboard motor attached, that was turning in toward shore. A boy with bright red hair sat at the tiller and he seemed to be directing the boat in toward the dock.

Neil uttered an exclamation of disgust and started hurriedly for the road.

"Where are you going?" Jan called.

"You can have him!" Neil said over his shoulder. "I won't stay around for *his* company!" And away he went at a jogging trot toward the house next door to the Pendletons'.

Apparently that was a favorite phrase of Neil Kent's, Jan thought. He was always "giving" it, him, or them— to anyone who would "have" them. She watched with new interest as the boy in the dinghy came skillfully in to tie up at the dock. Looking down as he made fast the rope, she saw that he was the dirtiest boy she had ever beheld in her life. There were generous streaks of black on his once white shirt, and more of it on his jeans. His hands were black and there were patches of black rubbed along one side of his face. Probably his red hair was full of the stuff too, because he did not hesitate to wipe a hand through it before he bent to pick up a large electric fan that he lifted to the dock. Then he climbed out of the boat himself and stood for a minute looking after the retreating figure of Neil Kent.

"Good riddance!" he said, and turned his attention

severely upon Jan. "And in case you're thinking of getting into my boat while I'm gone — don't."

Jan could only gape in astonishment. Certainly she had no intention of climbing into his greasy old boat, and she couldn't see why he should warn her so rudely against such action. Before she could find words to answer him, he had picked up the fan and started off toward shore.

As she stared after him, Jan saw that the bearded young man had not left the vicinity after all. He was standing near the Pendleton house, half concealed by a clump of hydrangea bushes. When the red-haired boy neared him on his way along the road, the watcher stepped back, disappearing from sight behind the bushes.

Jan sighed and turned away from the scene. It was not her affair and she had seen enough of rude boys and mysterious watchers. There were other things she wanted to think about.

2 THE MAN
ON THE STAIRS

JAN WANDERED OUT to the end of the dock, where the warm sun had already dried boards that had been rain-soaked during the night. She sat down as Neil had done, swinging her legs above water that lapped gently around the pilings of the dock. At least her meeting with Neil had banished the homesick feeling for a little while. But the moment she was alone, it all came sweeping back in a wave, ready to engulf her in misery. Perhaps she could hold the feeling off if she thought about what her father had told her of her great-grandmother.

Recently Dad had made a trip to Washington to be briefed on his work in Vietnam, and then he had come to Connecticut to visit his mother and grandmother.

"I'm worried about Miss Althea," he told Jan when he returned to California. At some time or other during his growing-up years Dad had started calling old Mrs. Pendleton "Miss Althea" as a sort of pet name. She had liked it and from that time on his grandmother had always been "Miss Althea" to her favorite grandson.

"She has difficulty walking," Dad went on, "and she can't manage stairs anymore. She stays on the upper floor of that old house and never goes out at all. She lives too much in the past, so that she's shut off from every-thing that's happening in the world today. She doesn't care for television—she says she prefers her own thoughts. And she doesn't even turn the radio on very often."

Mom was listening at the time and she shook her head doubtfully. "Perhaps Miss Althea has earned the right at her age to enjoy the past, and ignore the present. Old people often do that, you know."

Dad would not accept such reasoning. "Not my Miss Althea! When you get so tired of life that you stop being involved in it, you turn into a vegetable. Her mind is as keen as ever and I hate to see her lose interest in living. As a boy I always considered her a person of great vitality, a person who possessed the secret of inner hap-piness. Now she's no longer happy and this is a disturbing thing to see. Janice, perhaps you're the one who can wake her up and bring her back to caring about the present."

Such an assignment sounded alarming and Jan had looked her dismay. "I thought you said I wasn't to upset her," she protested. "I thought you wanted me to keep out of trouble."

"There's a difference between getting her interested in what is going on around her, and upsetting her," Dad said. "As a matter of fact, if she comes to life at all she's likely to upset you. She can be unexpected and discon-certing. She used to enjoy surprising people and making them think. Now she seems too apathetic for her own good. She was even dressed like an old woman when I saw her this time. She was all in black, and I scolded her for that. She used to be a regular bird of paradise in her dresses and hats."

Jan said nothing. This strange great-grandmother still

seemed too remote a person for her to have any real contact with.

Mom broke in with her own suggestion to Jan. "Of course there's that ugly old Chinese idol your father said used to haunt him as a boy. Isn't there some sort of mystery about him that you could investigate?"

Dad looked amused. "When I was young that ugly china figure fascinated me. He was a fat old boy with a face to give you nightmares. Miss Althea used to keep him on a high, dark shelf, with his face turned to the wall, so she wouldn't have to look at him. All of which convinced me that there must be a mystery about him. In fact, I spent some time trying to ferret it out whenever I visited the house. It's possible that—"

Suddenly he hesitated, as if he had remembered something. "On second thought, Jan, you'd better forget about Old Fang-Tooth. You could really upset Miss Althea if you pay much attention to him. I fancy she's had enough of that in her lifetime. Let the Chief Monster keep his secret—if he has one."

At any other time the way her father had drawn back from the subject and warned her to leave it alone might have offered tantalizing bait to Jan. But it had not interested her then because of the looming problems in her life. Nor did it interest her now while she was in so despondent a mood. What did she care about a silly old Chinese idol? The empty hollow of longing inside her was all that could really hold her attention. She sat on the end of the dock swinging her legs and aching with the emptiness of missing her family.

"Janice? Janice—where are you, dear?"

That was her grandmother's voice and Jan got to her feet, glad to be called away from her own gloomy thoughts. She answered the call and ran toward the Pendleton house. As she climbed the bank she noted that the man with the beard had disappeared from beyond the hydrangea bushes and seemed to be nowhere in sight.

Gran was waiting for her on the porch. She was a small, pretty woman—not at all old-looking. Her hair was brown and she wore it in a curly fluff about her face. Her eyes reminded Jan of her father's—gray and steady and cheerful. A year or so ago Gran had retired from her work in a public library, but since she had not wanted to be away from books, she had taken a position in the bookstore in the Seaport across the river. Since the shops and exhibits did not open until ten o'clock, she was still at home this morning.

"I see you've already made some friends," she said as Jan came up the steps.

She sounded pleased and Jan was sorry to disappoint her. "Not really. The boy next door wasn't very friendly. And that dirty, red-haired boy was awfully rude. He scowled at me and told me to stay out of his boat. As if I'd want to get into the dirty old thing!"

Gran had a rather odd look on her face. She seemed to be staring at something just beyond Jan. With a sinking feeling Jan turned and there was the red-haired boy right behind her—where, of course, he had heard every word. Beyond him Mrs. Marshall, the housekeeper, stood in the doorway, and her cheeks looked a little pink.

Jan tried to tell herself she didn't care, but she felt thoroughly uncomfortable. Gran did her best to mend the silence with words.

"Janice dear, I want you to meet Mrs. Marshall's son Patrick. He is just about your age, and—and I had hoped you would be friends."

Under the circumstances this didn't seem likely, but Jan managed a mumbled, "Hello," disliking the boy all the more because she felt so uncomfortable.

He returned her greeting curtly, clearly liking her no better than she liked him. "I thought you were a friend of Neil Kent next door," he said. "The first day he arrived he got into my boat without permission after I tied it up, and took it off upriver. I sure bawled him out when he came back."

Neil had no business doing that, Jan thought, but the fact did not make her like Patrick Marshall any better.

"I don't know anything about boats," she said stiffly.

Patrick shrugged and returned his attention to the electric fan he had brought up to the house. When he knelt beside it, he was completely hidden by a chair, as he must have been when Jan first came up the steps. Mrs. Marshall stood in the doorway looking flushed and unhappy.

Vainly Jan wished that she could start all over and come up the steps again without saying anything so unfortunate in Patrick Marshall's hearing. Not because she cared what he thought, but because she had upset Gran and the boy's mother. She had no wish to hurt their feelings. Besides, if she was to make no trouble and be welcome in this house, the main rule was not to be a disturbing element.

"Your great-grandmother is willing to see you this morning," Gran said. "In a little while you may go upstairs and talk to her for a few minutes."

Willing to see you did not sound friendly, and Jan felt increasingly ill at ease. Why couldn't they let the old lady alone if she didn't want to be bothered with great-grandchildren?

"Mother seems a little upset about something this morning," Gran continued. "I'm not sure this is a good time for her to see you, but—"

Suddenly Jan remembered what Neil had told her and she broke in, her words sounding more abrupt than she intended. "Was there a burglary here last night?"

Gran's eyes widened in startled amazement. "How did you know? We haven't said a word to anyone. Mother only mentioned a little while ago that something was missing. How could you possibly—"

Jan explained quickly. "Neil Kent—the boy who lives next door—saw someone on the outside stairs during the storm last night. A man in yellow oilskins. He was carrying something and behaving in an odd sort of way."

Patrick stopped working on the fan and shoved the chair aside so he could see Jan. Behind him Mrs. Marshall, plump and motherly, looked a little frightened. Gran was plainly disturbed.

"Then something was taken?" Jan asked.

"I—I don't know," Gran faltered. "That is—we're not sure."

"What is it that's missing?" Patrick asked bluntly.

Gran managed a stiff smile. "Oh, nothing important. Just a funny old Chinese idol that once belonged to my grandfather, Gillespie Osborn. It has no particular value and I can't imagine why anyone would take it."

Patrick stopped staring and became very busy with the fan again, getting it and himself a bit more smeary as he worked. Mrs. Marshall made a small, frightened sound and scurried out of sight into the house.

Gran said, "Never mind. Let's not worry about it now."

But Janice Pendleton was very busy worrying. If this

was the ugly old idol her father had told her about, more might be happening than Gran was ready to believe. The mystery no longer seemed so remote and stale. It had moved very close. If someone had been interested enough to climb Great-grandmother Althea's stairs at night during a bad storm and had taken that idol—this was mystery here and now. Another thing seemed strange— no one had questioned her about the man on the stairs, or even wanted to know more about what Neil had seen. It was as if all three—Gran, Mrs. Marshall, and Patrick— wished she would stop talking about what had happened.

She could not stop. This was too important a matter to drop so carelessly. Probably they didn't recognize how important it was, having no interest in the idol.

"Have you told the police?" she asked.

"Oh, we wouldn't want to do that," Gran said a little too quickly. "It's not as though we're absolutely sure any- thing is missing. Sometimes Mother forgets where she puts things. The figure will probably turn up right where she tucked it away."

"But Neil Kent saw—" Jan began.

"*Him!*" said Patrick Marshall explosively. "I wouldn't believe anything Neil Kent said on a bet!"

Gran was growing more nervous. "Yes—well—uh—I don't think we will do anything right away, Janice dear. I must get along to the bookstore or I'll be late."

"I can run you across in my boat," Patrick offered. "This fan is O.K. I don't think you'll have any more trouble."

Gran smiled at him doubtfully. "If your boat is as greasy as you are, Patrick, I think I'll rely on my car. Wouldn't you like to wash up before you go?"

"No, thanks," Patrick said and rubbed a new grease streak on his chin.

Gran started toward the steps. "Jan, if you'd like to come over to see some of the exhibits and meet me at the bookstore for lunch, it will be fine. Perhaps Patrick can run you across. After you visit your great-grandmother, of course. About the visit, dear — don't stay too long. She isn't used to children anymore, and besides, she is more accustomed to boys than girls. All her children and grand-children were boys. So you are something new in her experience. She will tire quickly, so go up and meet her and come down as soon as you can. And — ah — I don't think I'd mention anything about that idol, if I were you."

She said a hurried good-by to Jan and to Patrick and his mother, and went down the steps and around the house toward the garage. Mrs. Marshall went inside and Jan stepped to the porch rail to watch as Gran backed the car out and drove off down the road with a wave of her hand. Where downtown began, Jan knew, there was a bridge and Gran could cross it to the other side where the Seaport and the exhibits were, as well as the bookstore that specialized in nautical and New England lore.

Behind her, Patrick spoke gruffly. "I've got an errand to do for Pop — it'll take me an hour or so. Then I can come back and clean up and take you across in my boat, if you like."

Since she had no idea how she would get across the river otherwise, Jan said, "Thanks," somewhat re-luctantly. Everything about this boy seemed to rub her the wrong way, including the way he was so ready to dislike her. She felt like arguing with him simply because he made her feel prickly.

"I think Neil did see somebody on the outside stairs last night," she insisted. "He wasn't making it up. He pointed out the same man down there on the road this morning."

With his face so smeared with grease, it was hard to read Patrick's expression, but she knew she had caught his interest.

"What man? What did he look like?" he demanded roughly.

Jan described the man she had seen. "Dark-haired and thin. Maybe about my father's age, so not really old. Growing a beard on his chin."

There was something almost frightening about Patrick Marshall's intensity. "When was this? When did you see this fellow?"

"A little while ago," Jan told him. "He was there when you brought that fan up from your boat. He was behind the hydrangea bushes watching you all the time."

Patrick took the porch steps in two strides and raced toward the big bushes with the lavender-blue flowers. At the same moment, from the corner of her eye, Jan saw someone come out on the veranda of the house next door. When she turned to look she saw that Neil Kent stood there, scowling. When Patrick gave up his search — the stranger had clearly gone — and returned to his boat, Neil went inside, slamming the screen door behind him.

Jan watched as the red-haired boy cast off and chugged away on the errand for his father. She wished that her grandmother had mentioned some other way to get across the river. She did not want to be taken anywhere by Patrick Marshall.

From upstairs a sound floated through the open windows — the soft bong-bong-bonging of a gong struck on three separate musical notes. Inside the house she heard Mrs. Marshall hurrying up the stairs. In a few moments Patrick's mother was back, looking out the front door at Jan.

"That was her signal," Mrs. Marshall said. "Old Mrs.

Pendleton will see you now. You run along up. And remember what your grandmother said — don't stay too long
and tire her."

Hesitantly Jan went into the house. The hallway
seemed dark after the bright morning sunlight outside.
The stairs were old-fashioned and rather steep and narrow, with worn carpeting down the center. Jan took hold
of the polished mahogany banister as she climbed, and
wished that her heart wouldn't thud so much. There was
no reason to be afraid of this very old relative. There
was no reason to feel so nervous.

Nevertheless, she was short of breath by the time she
reached the upper hallway and stood facing a door that
was slightly ajar. Beyond, the old lady awaited her and
Jan's picture of her was very clear in her mind. Once at
home she had been taken to visit an old lady of nearly
ninety, wizened and sharp of face, and so shrunken that
she seemed to rattle around in her musty black clothing.
She had worn ugly, stubby shoes and her skimpy hair
had been pulled straight back in a style that took as little
effort as possible. Some of her teeth were missing and
she had made horrid little mouthing noises most of the
time. Jan had found herself looking at her as something
strange and foreign, not to be understood by a girl of
twelve. She braced herself for a similar experience. The
only difference was that the old woman she was about to
face was her own relative, and she could not escape her
and stay away for good. She remembered her father's
reference to a vegetable existence and found that all the
more unappealing.

"Well, come in, come in! What are you standing out
there for?" demanded a surprisingly clear, unwavering
voice.

Thus bidden, Jan advanced to the door and pushed it

wide. So great was the contrast of the room before her with anything she had seen in the rest of the house, that she stood for a moment in the doorway, stunned by the impact of color and texture and scent upon her receptive senses. She was aware of Chinese carpets, faded to a tawny wheat color and bordered with a pattern of Oriental figures in blue and rose. She was aware of a great fireplace facing the door, with shining brass andirons before it, and a pink marble mantel above. Brass candlesticks stood at each end of the mantel with tall candles in them, and between them stood small ornaments of porcelain and ivory on teakwood stands. Over the mantel hung the painting of a lovely Chinese scene in which mountain peaks and waterfalls seemed to tumble in rippled lines high above the small human figure that climbed upward over steep brown rocks.

As all this rushed upon her in a blur of bright impressions, she was at the same time aware of a single vivid splash of color far to her right down the long room. She turned toward it as if drawn by a magnet and faced the astonishing figure of her great-grandmother, Althea Pendleton.

3 GREAT–GRANDMOTHER ALTHEA

THE OLD LADY stood waiting for her, propped firmly between two canes. She was slender and fairly tall and she wore a long gown of rippled Chinese silk of a warm raspberry color. Her white hair dipped in little waves at each temple and was wound into a loose coil at the back of her neck. But all this was merely a setting for the focal point — a face of beauty and dignity. True, her skin was too pale, and the wrinkles were many, but Althea Pendleton's chin line was strong, her nose thin and aristocratic, with a slight beak at the bridge. Her eyes were so deep-set, so lost in their hollows, that it was hard to know their color at first glance. Her eyebrows were strongly arched, and perhaps touched with a pencil to retain the character of their dark marking. She had troubled to dress herself to receive the company about to call upon her — which did not seem at all the act of a vegetable.

The searching look from deep-set eyes was so disconcerting that Janice found herself blinking and shifting her own gaze to her great-grandmother's feet. These too were worthy of note, for she wore black velvet slippers embroidered with tiny flowers outlined in white pearls and threads of brilliant color.

The silence grew long and awkward and still Althea Pendleton did not speak. When she could not bear the quiet any longer, Jan said, "H-h-hello," hating the way she stammered.

The old lady responded with no expected greeting. In the same clear, unwavering voice she merely asked a question: "Who are you?"

Jan's look sped back to her face in astonishment, but there was no smile there. Had her great-grandmother forgotten who she was in the time since she had rung the gong and Janice had been sent upstairs? Perhaps it was like that with very old people.

"I'm Janice Pendleton," Jan managed. "I'm Bob Pendleton's daughter."

"Of course. I know that," Mrs. Pendleton said. "But that merely identifies you. I am asking a question much more important."

Jan hadn't the slightest notion what this old lady meant. She only knew that the tall, arresting figure before her held her interest completely, and frightened her not a little, as well.

Mrs. Pendleton made a slight movement, balancing herself between her two canes. "Since you've lost the power of speech, let's turn the question around. Who do you think I am?"

It was clear that if Jan announced that Mrs. Pendleton was her great-grandmother, she would be told that this too was the wrong answer. The difficulty of understanding what this old lady meant was growing rapidly worse, but it was also becoming a little funny. Jan suppressed a giggle that made her prickle with embarrassment. Surely no one would ever dare to giggle at Mrs. Pendleton. A thought had popped unbidden into Jan's mind, and

however flustered she felt, she tried to find the words
that would express it.

"I think you must be someone out of *Alice's Adventures in Wonderland*."

Wrinkled, heavily veined lids closed briefly over
sunken eyes. Then Mrs. Pendleton turned her head a
little so that sunlight from a window touched her face,
and when she opened her eyes Jan saw the green shine
of them — almost like the twinkle of an emerald.

"If you tell me that I remind you of the Duchess with
her squalling brat, I shan't be pleased," Mrs. Pendleton
said.

This time Jan really giggled, but she wasn't laughing
at this formidable woman. "Oh, no — never the Duchess!
And you're not the Queen of Hearts, or the untidy White
Queen. Perhaps it's because this is a Wonderland sort of
room, so you must belong here — whoever you are."

"Good for you!" the old lady said. "I suppose I ought
to be put right through the looking glass for giving you
such a welcome. You can't possibly know who I am —
and you are much too young to know who you are. I was
only playing games to confound you and see how you
would react. Come here by the window, Janice Pendleton, and let me see you better."

Thus bidden, and feeling less frightened, though still
confused, Jan stepped into the room and went to her
great-grandmother's side. The raspberry silk gave out a
spicy scent, and Jan, who had once owned a cast-off
sandalwood fan of her mother's, recognized the pleasant
odor. Great-grandmother continued to stare with her
green gaze that missed little, for all that she wore no
glasses.

"Only the very old may stare with impunity, Janice.

So you will permit me this privilege. Do you know what the word 'impunity' means?"

Jan nodded. "I think it means that you do something you shouldn't do and get off without punishment."

The faintest hint of a smile appeared at one corner of her great-grandmother's mouth. "Fair enough. That is a point scored for you. So now perhaps we are even. Not a bad beginning, you know. At my age I mistrust children—especially girl children. And you undoubtedly mistrust anyone as ancient as I. We'd still be looking at each other doubtfully across the years if I hadn't taken a shortcut, and if you had not responded."

That was true, Jan thought. Some sort of unexpected ease had been established between them. It was as if she and this very old lady had reached out and touched each other briefly, so that they were no longer entirely strangers.

Suddenly Mrs. Pendleton exclaimed, "I'm tired! I can't stand so long propped on these horrid canes!" Her voice startled Jan. It was suddenly plaintive and revealed a quaver of age that had not been evident before. She moved uncertainly to take her great-grandmother's arm, but Mrs. Pendleton shrugged her aside and managed the few steps to a big armchair, lowering herself carefully into its welcoming depth.

"There—that's better! Sit wherever you like, child. But close, so that I can see you."

The invitation meant exactly what it said, so Jan dropped cross-legged onto the soft Chinese rug, sitting on the floor not far from her great-grandmother's chair. The old lady leaned back and closed her eyes, resting for a few moments.

It did not seem fair to stare at her when her eyes were closed, so Jan stole a look around the room instead.

Everything in it was interesting and seemed to have come from faraway places. It was a double room, actually stretching from the front of the house to the back. The furniture was graceful and old-fashioned, the sofa upholstered in pale-gold damask. From the center of a white plastered arch that separated the front of the room from the rear, hung a many-sided Chinese lantern, with ladies and gentlemen in Oriental garments painted in bright colors upon frosted glass. Nearby was a low carved table of some dark wood, with a mother-of-pearl design set into the top. In a far corner stood a huge cabinet, its carved doors closed and a little gold key in the lock. Toward the front of the room was another cabinet, this one of glass, with glass shelves within, on which was displayed a fascinating array of small figures and ornaments.

Though she looked carefully all around, Jan could find nothing that resembled a fat and ugly Chinese idol. In a far, dark corner of the room was the place, she was sure, where it belonged. A triangular shelf had been set high into corner walls, just as her father had described. The shelf seemed meant to hold a fairly large squat figure. But there was nothing upon it, and when she turned back to her great-grandmother, she found the old lady regarding her thoughtfully. In spite of herself, Jan flushed—as if Mrs. Pendleton might have read her thoughts, sensed her curiosity about the missing figure. Quickly Jan pretended interest in an array of chessmen set out on a chessboard table. To cover her confusion she picked up a red knight and saw that it was a robed Chinese gentlemen riding a horse and carrying a lance.

"The red ones are carved from cinnabar," her great-grandmother said. "The white are ivory. And have you ever seen scrimshaw, child? Look at this." She reached for one of her black canes and held the head of it toward Jan. "That was carved from the tooth of a sperm whale. My husband — your great-grandfather, Captain Randal Pendleton — carved it long ago on one of his voyages."

The carving was exquisitely done in the shape of an ivory hand — a graceful feminine hand with a carefully detailed ring on the little finger.

"He made it for a paperweight," Mrs. Pendleton said. "He didn't know that I would have it set upon the head of a cane when he had been so long lost at sea, and I was as old as time itself."

The head of the other cane was a little cat, and both made firm and decorative handles. Jan studied the carvings solemnly, saddened by her great-grandmother's words.

A sudden change of tone in the old lady's voice startled her. "Enough of that. Your father wanted you to come here and get acquainted with the past. Mystic, Connecticut, is a modern town in many ways, but it is also the very old past. Did you want to come?"

The green eyes no longer seemed shadowed. They regarded Janice with a look that demanded the truth and no polite evasions.

"No," Jan admitted. "I didn't want to come. I wanted to be with my mother and the twins in Okinawa. I wanted to be with my family." She remembered too late that Gran and Mrs. Pendleton were also family, but the old lady did not seem to notice.

"Yes — I can understand that better than you think. I was only a few years older than you are when my mother died. I was living in Shanghai at the time and that was all the life I knew — my father's home and a convent school I went to. I didn't want to be separated from my father and sent home to the United States, which I'd never seen at all. But my father insisted and I was sent to a young lady's school in Boston, where some of my relatives lived."

She paused, thinking back to that long ago time. Jan spoke into the silence.

"I would hate that too. I'd rather stay here than be sent away to school."

Her great-grandmother went on as though she had not heard. "I hated it even more than I've hated giving up the world and retiring to these upstairs rooms because my knees have grown treacherous and no longer get me around. At least old people can give things up more easily than the young."

Jan's eyes roamed the beautiful, fascinating room—and saw it for the first time as a prison. This was not, she thought, the sort of choice she would make in her great-grandmother's place.

"Why do you stay up here?" she asked. "Doesn't more of the world come in downstairs? Couldn't you go out once in a while if you lived down there?"

The old lady took up her canes and pulled herself to her feet. "Come," she said. "I'll show you what I have up here."

She walked fairly well if she did not have to move far, and if she moved slowly. Jan walked at her side, knowing better now than to touch her or offer help. The front windows of this wing of the house made a wide opening that looked out upon the green branches of trees. But the trees were on either side and did not hide the view. From this high place the river was visible, and the white buildings and ships of Mystic Seaport on the opposite shore.

"Do you see?" Mrs. Pendleton gestured with one cane. "Here I have the sky with all its changes, and the water that reflects them. I can watch the sailboats on the river where I used to sail. I can dream and remember. Downstairs there is cooking and eating and the business of everyday living. I am remote from that up here. I can be alone—and I do not mind being alone. Nothing can reach me or trouble me here. Why should I want to go out in noisy, dirty traffic? Why should I have to worry about the downstairs world? I like it better here."

She opened a door to the upper porch that was reached by the outside stairs and stepped through it into open air and the touch of dappled sunlight.

"I have this too. I am not shut indoors. Even in the wintertime I can be outside for as long as I wish. I have no need of distant places anymore."

In a way, Jan felt, she could understand. And yet—to be shut away from all the bustle and activity and *doing* that existed down there on the earth—that seemed a terrible thing.

"How can you bear it?" she asked, speaking her thought.

Mrs. Pendleton smiled a little sadly. "All our lives we come to times when we must give up something we have cared about. Often this only means that we've grown a little and are ready for something new. I can remember very well how much I loved to play with paper dolls when I was a little girl. I couldn't bear the thought of ever having to stop playing with them. Yet when the time came, it didn't hurt at all. I hardly even noticed because they had begun to bore me and there were other, more interesting things to substitute."

Jan considered this. It was a comforting idea, in a way. Yet there was a question she had to ask.

"Is there something more interesting to substitute now?"

Her great-grandmother closed her eyes and said nothing for a long moment.

"You sound like your father, who doesn't approve of my choice. But perhaps I am old and tired. All I want is to be quiet, to rest. So don't you dare say, 'like a vegetable.' Your father pricked me with that. Though thanks to his pricking, I've at least stopped wearing black clothes. I've dressed up for his daughter in one of my silk robes from Hong Kong."

Jan smiled at her shyly and then leaned on the porch rail to look down into the Pendleton front yard. At once her attention was caught. The man with the sprouting beard was down there near the front steps talking to Mrs. Marshall. Patrick's mother seemed more worried and upset than ever. She spoke in a low tone to the young man and her words could not be heard up here. After a moment she turned and ran up the steps into the house, and as she did so Jan glimpsed her tear-streaked face.

She glanced quickly at her great-grandmother and saw that the old lady had also witnessed the little scene below. She stood at the rail beside Jan and stared down into the yard at the man who was now alone. He must have felt their attention upon him, for he looked up suddenly and saw them there. At once a wryly mocking smile lifted the corners of his mouth.

"Good morning, Mrs. Pendleton," he said and gave her a salute.

The old lady turned from the rail without speaking, and the thin young man went off down the road in the direction of town. Mrs. Pendleton stood with her back to lawns and trees and river, resting stiffly on her two canes, not looking after him.

"I only want to be left alone," she said to herself.

"I'm too old to be troubled anymore with other people's problems. I've lived through all the times of trouble and suffering that I want to. I'm entitled to peace."

"Who is he?" Jan asked softly, feeling she had to know.

Mrs. Pendleton started, as if she had forgotten the presence of her young visitor. "It isn't who he is that matters. It is what he has become. And about that I'm not sure. I think it's very likely that he has turned into a scoundrel, though once upon a time when he was a little boy, I loved him dearly."

"I saw him watching the house early this morning," Jan said. "Neil Kent, the boy next door, says he saw him on your stairs last night during the storm. Neil says he was carrying something in his arms as he came down."

The look of pain on Mrs. Pendleton's face turned to indignation. "Apparently no one has told you the rules, Janice! Apparently no one has warned you that old Mrs. Pendleton is not to be troubled or worried or frightened. She is to be kept in cotton batting and preserved for — for what? I ask you, child — for what?"

Jan could only stare in bewilderment. Somewhere she had lost the thread of this conversation. Her great-grandmother saw her expression and relented.

"Never mind, child. Now that we know the rules other people make for us, we'll go inside and you can tell me all about this Neil boy next door and what he thinks he has seen."

Jan, feeling no less bewildered, held the door open for her great-grandmother as the old lady went through.

"I thought you didn't want to be troubled with other people's problems," she said. "I thought you just told me — "

Mrs. Pendleton answered tartly. "Never remind me of anything I've just said. If I ever get to the place where I can't change my mind, I will be really old. Perhaps your father's right and it's a rule of life that we can never be let alone, no matter how carefully we draw apart, or however much others try to protect us. That young man in the yard came to see me last night. I didn't ask him to. I sent him away and washed my hands of his problem. But whether I like it or not I seem to be involved because he has taken something of mine. Tell me what this boy next door said."

"He thought the man he saw was a thief. Neil says everybody knows you have a Chinese treasure."

Mrs. Pendleton had lowered herself into her big armchair once more, and once more Jan sat cross-legged on the floor in front of her.

"Treasure!" the old lady echoed. "It's hardly that anymore. The most valuable things in my father's collection had to be left in China when I fled for my life. He sent out some of his porcelains well ahead of the trouble. When the rebellion came I could bring away only those small pieces of jade that were easy to carry in my handbag. Only one large piece was brought out at that time, and it was no choice of mine."

It seemed to Jan that her great-grandmother's gaze flicked briefly in the direction of that high, triangular shelf in the corner.

Jan spoke softly. "Neil couldn't see what the man was carrying last night when he came down the stairs, but Gran says the Chinese idol is missing."

Mrs. Pendleton looked suddenly cross. Her deep-set green eyes sparked with annoyance. "So what if it is? I always hated the old thing. It has sat up there in its corner for so many years, reproaching me constantly. Or it would have, if I hadn't turned its face to the wall. Last night I said to Eddie, 'Go away and don't bother me.' And I went out of this room and left him here. He left, but he took *that* with him. He must have. There's been no one else here except your grandmother and Mrs. Marshall. But let's forget about him. I don't want all those old stories to start up again. If you'd like to see what is left of Gillespie Osborn's famous jade collection, go over to the cabinet and open the door."

Jan got up from the carpet and went toward the tall cabinet with the carved doors with the little gold key in the lock. But before she could touch the key the old lady stopped her.

"No—not that one! That's where I hide the monsters. It's better if they don't see the light of day. I mean the glass cabinet beyond. Look over the jade pieces and pick out one that interests you. Then bring it here and we'll talk about it. My father had what the Chinese call 'jade madness.' He was obsessed with the collecting of jade."

Carefully Jan opened the glass doors and looked at an array of small figures on the shelves—all carved from jade. They were made, not only of green jade, with which she was familiar, but from jade of every soft color and mixed shading imaginable.

"I didn't know jade came in so many colors," Jan said.

"It does indeed. And the Chinese have fascinating names for the colors. Some of the greens are called king-fisher, spinach, emerald, moss, and my favorite, young onion green. That old ivory color they call chicken-bone. Pure jade is white, you know. The coloring comes from minerals. Today its value is increasing as sources are exhausted. Unless new veins are found somewhere in the world, there will eventually be no more new jade at all. Come—bring me a piece that interests you."

Jan's fingers moved uncertainly past a prancing ivory-colored horse, touched a small green dragon, a yellow bowl, and a little pink Buddha, to rest at last upon a lady of jade. She was about two inches high and made of green jade shaded with white. The piece felt pleasantly smooth and cool in Jan's fingers as she picked it up to examine it more closely. The lady's robes were carved in lovely, flowing detail, her face was serene, and a benign smile touched her lips. In her tiny hands she held a lotus blossom.

Mrs. Pendleton nodded as Jan brought the figure to her. "A good choice—one of my father's best pieces. That is Kwan Yin, Goddess of Mercy to the Chinese." She took the small figure and turned it appreciatively about in her fingers, then gave it back to Jan.

"Jade, like pearls, must be handled and loved. Its luster increases when it is touched. The Chinese say that it is calming to the spirit to hold a piece of jade in the fingers when one is disturbed. They believe jade has a spiritual quality that can transfer itself to man and heal his spirit. They call it the Stone of Heaven. So I don't lock my jade away. I want it to be enjoyed, not kept somewhere in a vault. My daughter worries about my being robbed, but who would wish to trouble an old lady like me? Jade is the symbol of happiness and these pieces used to make me happy—just as they did my father. Though sometimes I miss my Joyful Mountain."

Jan would have asked what she meant, but the old lady closed her eyes and leaned her head back against a velvet cushion. Her face seemed suddenly still and pale. Guiltily Jan remembered that Gran and Mrs. Marshall had both told her not to stay up here for very long. She had lost all sense of time, and now she had tired the old lady beyond her strength. Quickly she tiptoed to the cabinet and would have placed Kwan Yin on her shelf, but behind her Mrs. Pendleton's voice spoke faintly.

"Don't put her away. Let her stay out and enjoy the world. Put her on that table near the porch window where she can stand in the sun."

Jan did as she was bidden and returned to Mrs. Pendleton's chair. The old lady's eyes were closed again and her mouth looked drawn and pinched.

"Are you all right, Great-grandmother?" she asked in concern.

At once the green eyes looked at her. "Great-grandmother! That is such a long title to use. Shall we find some easier name for you to call me? Can you think of one?"

Jan nodded shyly. She had already thought of this before coming here, but she had not known if she would dare to use the name.

"I like what my father always calls you — 'Miss Althea.' Would you mind if I called you that?"

A blue-veined, wrinkled hand reached out and touched her lightly, almost affectionately. "Perhaps girls are nice too, though my children were all boys. I would like to have you call me that. The old friends who used to call me Althea are gone now. And to my new friends I'm Mrs. Pendleton. My father gave me that name — Althea — and I've always liked it. So use it, young Janice. Perhaps we will be good friends after all. Now run along and let me nap a little while."

Soundlessly Jan crossed the pale-gold carpet, softly she let herself through the door and closed it gently behind her. Her feet made hardly a sound on the stairs as she went down. She had left a magical world behind and she did not want to destroy the spell of it with any immediate clamor.

4 THE
HAPPY HEART

OUTDOORS THE MORNING sun was growing hot and Jan stood in the front yard watching the river. For the time she had been in Miss Althea's apartment, her sense of loss and homesickness had subsided a little. She had been so interested that her thoughts had been distracted from their forlorn course.

There was the curious matter of that old Chinese idol, for instance, and why the mysterious man with the beard had taken it away when Miss Althea had dismissed him. Jan could hardly wait to tell her friend Dorothy about all this. Then she remembered. There was no Dorothy to tell. It would take too long to put it into a letter, too long to get a reply. The hurt inside her, the emptiness, was returning like a toothache. Was it going to be like this every time she stopped for breath, every time she wasn't busy? If so, she must keep dizzy-busy all the time because she didn't want to be unhappy. She must go over to the Seaport and seek out the bookstore where Gran worked. She did not want to stand still long enough for those feelings to come again and hurt so dreadfully.

The dock below the house stood empty and there was no sight or sound of Patrick with his dirty, noisy little boat. Jan looked down at her clean, yellow dress and hoped she would not have to cross the river by that particular means.

A sound next door made her look around. A car was being started in the Kent garage. Neil came running down the steps and saw her there.

"Hey!" he called. "You want to go across? Mom's driving to town and she said she'd take me over to the exhibits. Nothing else to do around this place. You can come along if you like."

This seemed a friendly enough suggestion. "That would be fine," she called back. "Just a minute. I'll tell Mrs. Marshall I'm leaving."

She ran into the house and found Patrick's mother in the kitchen baking gingerbread. Her eyes looked pink from weeping, and Jan pretended not to notice.

"Mrs. Kent is driving over to the Seaport and Neil says they'll take me if I like," she said. "When Patrick comes back, will you tell him I got a lift?"

Mrs. Marshall promised to tell him and said she thought going in a car was more comfortable than in Patrick's boat anyway. "I suppose I shouldn't say that," she added. "Not when my husband runs a marina and boat service. Anyway, you go along with the Kents and I'll tell Patrick when he comes."

The car had backed out to the road and Mrs. Kent was waiting by the time Jan went outside again. She was a pretty, young-looking woman with very pale blond hair — even fairer than her son's. She had combed it rather carelessly, as though she had lost interest in her appearance this early in the day. Her blue eyes had an unhappy look about them, and her full red lips pouted a little.

"Hello," she said as Janice came into view. "Neil tells

me that he has found a new friend. I wish I could be as lucky."

The words sounded petulant and something Mom often said flashed into Jan's mind: "To have friends you have to *be* a friend. Nobody can resist that." Jan was not altogether sure this was true. Patrick Marshall would probably never even notice someone who was trying to be a friend. At least Neil was different, for all that he seemed a bit changeable.

As Jan came up, he opened the door and she got into the front seat next to his mother. Neil sat on the outside. Mrs. Kent's sandaled foot touched the gas pedal and the car moved down the road in the direction of the bridge across Mystic River.

Neil's mother drove as though other cars and other people had no right to get in her way. She seemed impatient and discontented, as though nothing at all pleased her. The few remarks she made caused Jan to feel uncomfortable and once or twice Jan glanced at Neil, understanding his own discouraged attitude a little better, since this was an example set by his mother.

The car left the bridge and the small shopping area of Main Street behind and followed the road that led through old Mystic, where, Gran had said, many of the original houses were still standing.

At least Neil found some things to be curious about. "Did you meet the old lady this morning?" he asked Jan. "Your great-grandmother, I mean."

Jan remembered the things he had said earlier and found herself eager to change his impression. "I've met her and I like her very much. There's nothing one bit spooky about her or about the Pendleton house."

"That's what you think," Neil said, unimpressed. "Did

she say anything about what was stolen?" he added.

"I don't know if anything was exactly stolen." Jan wanted to avoid the question. She was not at all ready to tell Neil what had come out of her visit with Miss Althea. "I think my great-grandmother knew the person who came to visit her last night."

Mrs. Kent's attention had been caught. "Stolen? Neil, do you mean there was a burglary in our neighborhood last night?"

"Don't get upset, Mom," Neil said quickly. "Maybe it was O.K. after all."

"Don't you start any of your play-acting around here," his mother said sharply. "We've had enough of that to last us a while." She braked the car and drew over to the side of the road. "I'll drop you across from the entrance, Neil. And I'll pick you up here at noon. Good-by now."

Jan found that she had been hurried out of the car and that Neil had grabbed her by the hand and hustled her across the road between the run of traffic. Once across, he turned to wave, but his mother had already driven on. Together he and Jan went to the ticket window to pay the small entry fee for children.

When they were through the gate Jan looked around with interest. This was like stepping back into a long ago New England world. All about were the winding streets and clapboard houses of a village — old houses, some of which had been brought from other places and reerected here to give an authentic flavor of the past. Above the rooftops Jan could see the masts of ships moored along wharves at the waterfront. That was an area she would especially like to explore, but first she must report to Gran.

"Do you know where the bookstore is?" she asked Neil.

"I'll show you," he said. "I have to go over to the clock shop. There's a man there I've been talking to and I want to see him again. Maybe he will help me out."

As they passed a small, white-towered meetinghouse, Jan glanced curiously at the boy at her side. For once there was lively interest in his blue eyes and he looked less like his mother.

"What do you mean—help you?"

Strangely, he seemed a little embarrassed. "Oh—it's about a hobby of mine. Maybe—if I get to know you better—you could help me too."

Jan remembered her mother's motto about being a friend and made an effort. "I'd like to help any way I can," she offered, and gave him her friendliest smile.

But Neil Kent was a strange boy who seldom responded as one might expect. He looked off into the distance and mumbled something she did not understand. Then he thrust out his chin almost as though she had offended him.

"I don't like to be laughed at," he said. "I don't like people who make fun of things I think are interesting."

Jan gaped in astonishment. "I didn't laugh. I don't even know what you're talking about, so how could I make fun of you?"

"You might," he said curtly.

There seemed no answer to that. Neil, quite clearly, was not going to respond to friendly gestures. They followed the curving sidewalk to the place where a cobble-stoned street cut across, and neither of them spoke again until Neil stopped to gesture.

"The bookstore is down this street, on a corner of the Village Green. You'll see the windows when you get there."

He was about to leave her, and Jan spoke hurriedly.

"Thanks for bringing me here. It was lots better than coming across in Patrick's boat."

"I should think so," said Neil ungraciously and scowled at her as if she had been Patrick himself.

"I didn't like him much either," she said. "But I don't know him yet. Why do you dislike him so much?"

"He thinks he owns everything around here," Neil growled. "He's bossy and rude. All I did was get into his old boat and try it out. I didn't know it was his."

"Maybe he thought you might fall overboard," Jan said.

"I'm probably a better swimmer than he is! No—all he cared about was that old dinghy. I know about boats and I wouldn't have hurt it. But he was sore. He acted as though I'd tried to steal the *Queen Elizabeth*."

This was not her quarrel, Jan felt. Probably both boys had behaved badly and without consideration, and she did not want to get into the middle of their fight.

When she said nothing, Neil gave her a sulky, "So long," and went off, leaving her unsure about both Neil Kent and Patrick Marshall as possible friends. She had never known two boys who were so difficult to figure out.

She sighed as she walked on toward the bookstore. On either side of the street small white and gray and yellow houses were open for inspection. Now and then down a side street she could glimpse the river. By letting her imagination go she could fancy herself a girl of an older day, living here in this old-fashioned village. There were no automobiles to break the illusion, though a horse-drawn dray went by with children riding in the cart. If only her friend Dorothy were here to enjoy this with her, or if this were only a vacation trip with Dad and Mom and the twins along!

That was the trouble with homesickness—it never let

you alone. Whatever you did it was waiting in the background to pounce the moment you gave it a chance. If she could just find someone she could talk to without being met by the scowls given out so easily by both Neil and Patrick.

She hurried a little to reach the bookstore and the everyday reality of her grandmother who, after all, was her father's own mother, and could provide some sense of family.

Jan could see the store ahead of her now — a building with a sloping roof. There was a sign outside and through the windows she could see books. She went quickly up the steps and into rooms in which she felt immediately at home. Books would make any place seem welcoming. On her left was a room with comfortable chairs, for browsing and reading. Books about sailing and whaling days were displayed on shelves all around. To her right was the bookstore proper, and here Gran was waiting on a customer.

On the drive to Mystic yesterday Gran had explained that a number of local men and women who had retired from other work kept busy and interested helping out at the Seaport. Some of them wore period costumes and told visitors about the buildings of which they were in charge. Gran did not dress up to sell books, though she did need to know all about her stock and what lay between the covers.

When Jan appeared, Gran left her customer to speak to her. "So you found me. At lunchtime we'll have a good visit and you can tell me about your morning. Right now I'm busy. Why don't you wander around outside for a while and come back when you're tired? Then we'll have lunch here on the grounds and talk. Perhaps you'd like to explore the waterfront. I'll give you a diagram map that will keep you from getting lost, and explain what you're looking at."

Jan took the yellow folder Gran handed her, but she must have seemed uncertain, for Gran slipped an arm about her as she took her to the door.

"One interesting place to see is the old rope walk down at the end of the waterfront. That's what they call a place where rope is made. Patrick's grandfather is usually around to explain things to visitors. Just tell Grandpa Marshall I sent you and he will make you welcome, I'm sure. That's what everyone calls him, so you might as well say 'Grandpa Marshall' too."

Jan was not certain that she wanted to talk to Patrick's grandfather. But since Gran had already returned to her customer and was busily answering questions, she wandered outside again.

There were not too many people walking about at the moment and the village streets dreamed in warm sunshine. White picket fences enclosed pocket-handkerchief-sized lawns, and trees had been planted along the sidewalks, providing shade and a haven for chirping birds. The streets were mostly unpaved — as the original dirt streets of such a village would have been.

Jan found her way to the waterfront — a wide, cobblestoned expanse that ran along the stone embankment. Near the water's edge white posts rose at intervals for the mooring of boats. Long wharves reached out into the river, with ships beside them. Some of the ships were old square-riggers, as Jan recognized from pictures in books of her father's. Dad had always been interested in ships and the sea. Visitors could go aboard these ships, and that promised to be interesting.

She passed the Printer's, the Weaver's, the Firehouse on the shoreside, moving slowly in the direction of Shipyard Point and the red, barnlike structure that cut across the end of the waterfront street. Everything was identified on the map Gran had given her and she studied it with mild interest.

The tall red structure ahead appeared to be a sail loft, and next to it was the long, low building of the rope walk. In every town along the seacoast where there had been shipbuilding the making of sails and rope had been important. As she knew from Dad, Mystic, with its safe harbor three miles inland from the sea, had once been a shipbuilding center, and shipsmith's shops and chandleries were all here to show those of later generations the way it had been in a bygone day.

Jan left the curve of the cobblestoned street and stepped off into sandy dirt. Hesitantly she approached the rope walk with its narrow entryway, but she did not at once mount the steps. Instead, she started down the out-side length of the building. She wasn't at all sure she wanted to go in and see Grandpa Marshall. What if Patrick was there, ready to scowl at her again?

She passed an exhibit of canoes and dugouts from Ghana and other distant places, and rounded the far end of the building, to find that there was a back door by which she could enter if she liked. Since it stood open she mounted the steps and looked in.

It was a little like looking down a long, dark tunnel. No one at all was in sight, though she heard distant voices from the far end as they came whispering through this

gloomy, echoing place. On her left the greater part of the long building was taken up by a bare floor. Strands of rope of various thickness ran the full length of the floor, with some sort of machinery at the far end. Outside this wire-enclosed section of floor ran a narrow corridor down which visitors might move. The tunnel made by this corridor would have been even darker, had it not been for patches of barred sunlight that fell across Jan's path from small-paned windows set in the outer wall of the building.

Still hesitant, but somehow drawn in spite of her doubts, Jan started down the corridor. Wooden boards creaked beneath her feet. Overhead slanted dark wooden beams, cobwebby and old. The air smelled of age, somehow, and her footsteps echoed hollowly along the bare boards.

Ahead, in the dim reaches of the front end, was a wooden structure that rose to an open loft above the machinery section. The voices she heard grew suddenly louder and the figure of a man started toward her out of the far darkness. He was almost running in his haste to reach the back door and as he brushed past Jan, she recognized the face with its fuzzy, dark beard and thick black hair. Once more this was the stranger who seemed to be haunting the Marshalls and who had been crossing her path all morning.

She drew back fearfully to keep from being knocked down as he dashed past, and stood with her back against the wire netting, looking after him in surprise. Apparently he had recognized her too, for after he had hurried by he wheeled and stood there in the gloom staring at her.

"Aren't you — ?" he began, but Jan gave him no chance to finish.

Suddenly she was afraid in this empty, lonely stretch of dark corridor. She knew with all her senses, if not with her reason, that this man spelled trouble. Trouble for Miss Althea and for the Marshalls. Perhaps trouble for herself if she stayed to listen to him. She turned and fled, her feet clattering noisily on old boards that groaned beneath her weight. She was making so much noise that she could not tell if he followed her, and she did not pause until she reached the front end of the building. Then she looked around and saw that he had disappeared. He must have gone outside through the back door, for he was nowhere in sight.

"Here, here now — what's all this noise?" said a gruff voice in her ear.

Jan was so nervous and unstrung that she jumped and might have fled back down the rope walk from this new menace, if a gnarled hand had not reached out and caught her by the shoulder. Terrified, she looked into the face of a little man not much taller than herself, but very tough and sinewy and strong. The clutch of his fingers on her shoulder revealed how strong he was.

"Children who come into the Seaport have to behave themselves," he told her. "You can't go dashing around as if you were on a playground at school."

His face was an angry red, but remembering the raised voices she had heard, Jan figured that his anger was not entirely for her. Gathering up her scattered courage, she looked into blue eyes that had a lively snap to them and tried to tell him what was the matter.

"I was scared," she said. "That — that man who ran out stopped and looked at me. And — and I don't like him. I was scared."

The gnarled hand let her shoulder go and the old man

closed his eyes for an instant as if something hurt him very much. "You're all right now," he said. "I'm sorry if I scared you too."

"I've been seeing him all morning," Jan rushed on. "Everywhere he turns up he seems to make people angry. Who is he anyway?"

The old man was dressed in clean, blue denim overalls and a blue shirt with rolled-up sleeves. He reached into a hip pocket of the overalls and pulled out a large blue bandanna with which he wiped his perspiring face. Then he blew his nose rather loudly. Jan had a feeling that all these elaborate motions were simply a delaying action — so that he wouldn't have to answer her question right away. But she really did want to know the identity of the disturbing stranger, so she persisted.

"Do you know who he is?"

The old man answered her gruffly. "That young fellow is no one I care to know, or even speak to. And I'd advise you to avoid him at all costs."

Jan had every intention of doing so, but the answer was far from satisfactory. The old man, however, turned to an exhibit of several tilted rows of spindles which held strands of hemp for the making of rope. He began to fiddle with them absently, as if waiting for her to go away.

"Are you — are you Grandpa Marshall?" she asked hesitantly.

He turned his sharp little chin and stared at her from beneath bushy eyebrows. "That's what they call me."

"I'm Janice Pendleton," Jan said. "My grandmother said I should stop in and see the rope walk, and — and meet you."

This time he looked at her with more interest. Some of the angry flush left by his encounter with the bearded young man had faded from his leathery brown skin.

Suddenly he gave Jan a surprisingly warm smile and held out his hand.

"So you're Bob Pendleton's daughter? Think of that now! I used to dandle Bob on my knee when he was half your size. And you're old Mrs. Pendleton's great-granddaughter too. I've known your family all my life, young lady. Good friends they've been to us. I've been making a little surprise for your great-grandmother in my spare time. Would you like to see?"

Jan nodded and Grandpa Marshall led the way up steep wooden steps to a wooden platform in the loft above. It wasn't exactly a second floor to the building, occupying only a portion of the upper space. The beams of the roof formed its ceiling, and it was open on all sides. Tacked against a post was a sign that read SPINNING ROOM, and there was indeed a spinning wheel on display, and other articles used in the making of rope. Here Mr. Marshall had set up a workbench and stool, and Jan saw that various tools and chisels for the carving of wood lay ready to hand. In the center of the workbench stood a partly completed model of a sailboat. Every detail of the hull and mast had been constructed with care, and Jan saw affection in Grandpa Marshall's eyes as he regarded the little boat.

"I've made fancier models than this," he said. "I've carved real ships in the days when I was a sailor. There's a model of the *Flying Cloud* I made on exhibit over in the museum. But this little boat means a lot to me. Clean and swift as a bird, she was. You can see her name on the hull, if you look."

Jan read the lettering aloud: "*Happy Heart.* What a lovely name for a boat! Was there a real boat by that name?"

"There was indeed," the old man said. "Young folks

used to sail her up and down the Mystic in the old days, and even out to sea. I can remember her — though your great-grandmother was a generation ahead of me and I was only a little boy at the time. This is a present for her — a surprise — so you're not to tell her what I'm making. She's been heartsick these days — being shut off from active life, with nothing but memories left. Perhaps this will make her smile again, and help her memories to be happy ones."

"I think that's wonderful," said Jan warmly. In spite of her first reception, she liked Patrick's grandfather. She need not have worried about meeting him after all. He wasn't in the least like his grandson, even though he could get furiously angry.

The old man seemed pleased with her words. He ran a fond hand over the hull and touched the name of the boat lightly.

"Why was it called the *Happy Heart*?" Jan wanted to know.

"I don't remember the whole story. Gillespie Osborn was a pretty smart fellow, I guess. He had a fine education and he wrote articles in his day for some of the best magazines. I suppose he was something of a philosopher, among other things. He wrote a piece once about having a happy heart. I suppose that's where Mrs. Pendleton got the idea for naming the boat. But now maybe you'd like to take a look around in here before you go? If you're interested, I can show you a few things."

Jan was interested and he took time to explain the rope walk to her, pointing it out from this high place as it stretched away below. He showed her how a man called the "spinner" first made the small yarns that were later combined to make ropes. He would wrap a "strike" of loose hemp fibers about his waist and hook a twist of this to the spinning head. Then as this head was revolved by a small boy turning a crank, the spinner would walk backward, feeding fibers from the strike around his waist into the constantly twisting and lengthening yarn. It was this operation that gave the building its name — the rope walk.

This particular rope walk had originally been 1,500 feet long, but when it was brought from Plymouth to Mystic it had been shortened to 250 feet. That still looked like a long way to walk backward, especially if one had to do it over and over all day long.

"Now machines do the work," Grandpa Marshall concluded, sounding a little regretful that this had to be so.

The morning was growing late, Jan realized, and Gran was expecting her for lunch, so she thanked Patrick's grandfather for showing her the *Happy Heart* and promised not to give the surprise away to Miss Althea. Then she climbed down the wooden ladder and went out the front door feeling much more cheerful than when she had entered.

That is, she felt cheerful until she saw the man who was waiting for her outside. Not far from the steps was a large stone horse trough with a hand pump beside it. Sitting on the rim of the trough, watching as Jan came down the steps, was the bearded stranger. When he saw her he stood up and moved toward her.

"Don't run away again," he said and there was an oddly urgent note in his voice. "There's something you can do for me, Janice Pendleton. How about walking along the waterfront with me a little way, so I can tell you about it?"

5 A NOTE
FOR PATRICK

JAN WOULD HAVE given anything to run inside the
rope walk again, but several visitors had just gone up the
steps and Grandpa Marshall was already busy greeting
them. She could hear his voice inside and knew that he
had not looked out the door to see who was waiting for
her.

"I—I've got to hurry back to the bookstore," Jan
faltered. "I'm late, and—"

"That's all right," the man said, falling into step beside her. "The bookstore is right on my way. And we
ought to get acquainted—you and I. Your father was my
good friend when we were boys and he used to come here
summers to visit. Though he was older, he never minded
when I tagged along. He was pretty swell—your father."

Jan threw her unwelcome companion a startled look,
but she had nothing to say. In his stories about Mystic,
her father had not mentioned the names of boyhood
friends, and somehow Jan did not trust this man. He
might be making all this up to get her on his side. Whatever his side was.

"Look," he said when he saw he could not win her
with talk of her father, "what I want you to do is easy

enough. This morning I saw you talking to Pat Marshall. Since his mother works for your grandmother, I know you'll see him again. All I want is for you to give him this note from me."

He had taken out a folded triangle of paper, sealed at one edge with a bit of cellophane tape, and held it out to her as they walked along. For a moment she regarded the note with acute distrust. Then she took it reluctantly and stopped on the walk to face the man beside her.

"Who are you? No one will tell me. What do you really want?"

"I'm the black sheep come home," he said, and though his smile mocked her, there was no laughter in his eyes. "They'd all prefer never to see me again. Except Pat. Maybe I can still count on him. He used to think a lot of his big brother. That's me. Just give him that note and tell him Eddie sent it. We'll see what happens next."

He did not wait for her agreement, but gave her a wry salute of finger to temple and went quickly off down a side street. Jan stood for a moment gaping after him in astonishment. Then she slipped the folded paper into the side pocket of her flared yellow skirt and hurried toward the bookstore.

Gran was sitting in the pleasant reading area, talking to a distinguished-looking, gray-haired gentleman. She held out her hand to Jan as she came in, and drew her into the circle of her arm.

"Mr. Chilton, this is my granddaughter, Janice," she said. And to Jan, "Mr. Chilton is curator of the museum here at the Seaport."

Mr. Chilton held out his hand to Janice and smiled at her approvingly. "I'm always glad to see a Pendleton come home to Mystic. Have you been looking around?"

"I've only visited the rope walk so far," Jan said shyly.

"Of course — that would be a natural place to go. The Marshalls and the Pendletons are old family friends, aren't they? Was Tom there — Patrick's grandfather?"

Jan nodded and Mr. Chilton did not pursue the matter further, but returned to his conversation with her grandmother.

"About this matter of Mrs. Pendleton's collection of Chinese jades and porcelains," he said, " — I do hope you will arrange for me to see her, or at least tell her of our request."

Gran had what she called a "worry dimple" near one corner of her mouth. It never showed when she smiled, but when she pressed her lips together in concern, the little dent appeared, indicating her state of mind. It was there now, Jan saw, as Gran regarded Mr. Chilton doubtfully.

"I'm not sure how Mother will take a request to show some of her jade pieces at the museum," she said. "These days, as you know, Mother seldom sees anyone and we try to protect her from outside worries and disturbances."

Listening, Jan thought of Miss Althea's words, and the way she had spoken of "the rules other people make for me." Dad, Jan thought, was not altogether in accord with those rules. He had thought Miss Althea needed more of an interest in the present. So why wouldn't showing some of her lovely things to others give her a connection with the outside world? But Jan could not speak such a thought to her grandmother, who knew Miss Althea far better than she did.

"At least you will ask her, won't you?" Mr. Chilton said. "We are planning a special exhibit of Oriental objects. The sort of things that clipper ships used to bring home in the days of the China run, when they made those amazingly fast voyages across the oceans. Gillespie Osborn was a part of that picture."

Gran nodded. "Most of the porcelain things Mother has were sent home ahead of time by Grandfather when he sensed that trouble was coming in China. But he couldn't bear to part with his jade pieces and he wouldn't let those go until the Boxer rebellion broke out. Then it was too late. He managed to send his daughter off to the safety of a Chinese friend's house, and she took with her as many of the smaller pieces as she could pack into her handbag. The larger things were left behind, of course, and Grandfather himself lost his life. Mother was smuggled out of the country to a British gunboat and was able to get away. So she brought her father's treasures back home with her."

"In a way," Mr. Chilton said, "that valuable jade would be safer locked in exhibit cases at the museum than it is in her possession."

"I'm quite sure you're right," Gran said, "but I wouldn't dare suggest that to Mother. She's a pretty strong-minded person, you know. In the end she will do exactly as she pleases. At least I'll pass along your request and find out if she will see you."

Mr. Chilton thanked her and told Janice he was glad to have met her. When he had gone, Gran left the store in charge of a woman who came in for the noon hour. Then she and Janice walked a short distance to the Pantry, a long, low, open building furnished with green picnic tables and benches.

When they had loaded paper plates and brought them back to one of the tables, Gran asked about Janice's

morning. Without further postponement, Jan plunged
into the matter of the note she had been given to deliver
to Patrick Marshall. She told about running into Eddie
Marshall several times, and of how he had waited for her
outside the rope walk. Then she showed Gran the folded
slip of paper.

"What do you think I'd better do? Nobody seems to
want him around. His mother was crying after he talked
to her. And his grandfather was angry. Miss Althea says
he is probably a scoundrel, and I think he stole something from her."

Gran listened gravely, sympathetically. The worry
dimple appeared beside her mouth, pressing its little dent
of concern into her cheek.

"I think you'd better give Patrick the note," she decided.

"That's what I'd like to do," Jan agreed. "It will be
up to him to decide about whatever is in it. But, Gran—
what's wrong with Eddie Marshall? Why doesn't anyone
want to talk about him?"

This time Gran's answer was evasive. "There was a
rather serious scandal, dear. Something disgraceful that
fine people like the Marshalls find hard to accept. Eddie
was always a bit wild and he got into trouble that was
inexcusable. He had to go away for a while. But the
thing is done with now and perhaps this town ought to
stop talking about it. Anyway, that is what I mean to do.
I don't know what steps Eddie means to take, since he's
come home, but I think the gossip about him ought to
stop."

After that Jan knew there would be no use asking
questions. Gran's attitude was probably right, but considering the size of Jan's growing curiosity, it was also

frustrating. She bit into her hamburger and for some time after that gave most of her attention to eating.

Not until she was finishing her ice cream did she return to the matter of the note she was to deliver.

"How can I find Patrick this afternoon?" she asked.

"There's an easy way—if he's there. He has been doing odd jobs all over this summer, and sometimes he works at the new marina his father has opened. Henry Marshall rents boats and works at repairing them and keeping them shipshape, as well as offering dock space and protection for those who want a place to leave their craft. I'm afraid he won't welcome Eddie's appearance on the scene. He may think having him around will give his place a bad name. But what I started to say is that you'll find the marina less than a mile upriver from here— right off Highway 27—the main road that runs past the Seaport. You can follow it until you come to the boat place. Be careful to walk on the side of the road and watch the traffic. If Patrick isn't there, perhaps his father can tell you where he is."

Right after lunch Jan set off to deliver the note. She walked in the grass along the roadside, with a ridge of low hills running along on her right, and the river not far away on her left. In the warm sun of noonday the walk might have seemed long, if it hadn't been that there was always something new along the road to look at. Around a curve, she came upon her destination unexpectedly.

A pebbly beach area ran down to the water, and there were small boats everywhere—some tied up at two little docks, or anchored in the sheltered curve that the river made nearby. Two or three were set up on chocks near a work shed. Down near the water a man with red hair— undoubtedly Patrick's father—was talking to the owner of a boat. Patrick himself, looking fairly dirty, but at least less greasy than he had earlier, was sanding the deck of a beached boat.

Jan called to him. It didn't matter if he scowled at her, she had an errand to perform. He looked down at her over the rail of the boat and of course he scowled at once.

"So you couldn't wait for me to take you across?" he jeered. "I suppose you thought Neil Kent's car was better than my boat?"

Jan prickled with resentment at his words. Probably he had not forgiven her for the things she had said in his hearing this morning.

"If you want to know—yes!" she told him. "Why should I want to go anywhere with as bad-tempered a boy as you are? At least Neil is a little more friendly."

The scowl did not diminish. It was as if Patrick Marshall had a permanent chip on his shoulder and was always daring somebody to knock it off.

"That's up to you," he said shortly and turned back to his work.

Jan drew the triangle of paper from her pocket and waved it at him. "I've brought you something. It's a note from your brother Eddie. He asked me to give it to you."

This time Patrick dropped his sandpaper and stood up. He threw a quick glance in his father's direction and vaulted over the rail of the boat, to drop to the beach beside Jan. He snatched the note from her hand and tore it open. She watched as his eyes traveled back and forth, reading the words eagerly. Apparently Eddie had been right. Patrick was still on his side.

When he looked at Jan again, the scowl had been replaced by an expression of excitement. "Thanks," he said, and actually smiled at her. His grin was a wide one

that not only showed his strong white teeth, but also bunched the freckles across the bridge of his nose. It gave him a rather impudent, surprisingly cheerful look.

Jan said, "You're welcome," somewhat stiffly and turned away. Just because he chose to smile at her now didn't mean that she would forgive his earlier rudeness.

"Hey, wait a minute!" he called as she started toward the road. "If you want to go across the river, I can take you right away. I'm going over. Come along, if you want."

As Neil had said, this boy was bossy. But if she did not accept his offer, she would have to walk back to Mystic and take her chances on finding a way to Gran's house. Without waiting to see if she would follow — probably because he didn't care — Patrick was already running down the beach toward his own boat, tied to the end of a dock. He spoke to his father as he went by, telling him he had an errand on the other side, and got into the boat.

Jan followed doubtfully. Except for rowboats in a park, she didn't know much about small boats, and she regarded this one doubtfully.

"Well, come on!" Patrick said. "That seat's all right — I cleaned off the grease." He held out a hand a bit scornfully and she climbed into the boat and sat down hurriedly on the crossboard he indicated.

Patrick started the motor and in a moment they were chugging off toward the opposite shore. Jan hung onto the seat with both hands and steadied herself against the slapping blows of the boat's prow against the water as its speed increased. She wasn't at all sure that this was a pleasant way to travel, but it was rather exciting. Patrick knew exactly what he was doing as he skirted other craft in crossing the river. On the opposite shore the row of captains' houses—built long ago in Mystic's seagoing days—stood up white along the shoreline, with the green of the hills rising behind. She could pick out the Pendleton house easily.

The little boat nosed toward the dock. As it approached, a man rose from the embankment and ran down to catch the rope Patrick tossed as the boat came in. It was Eddie Marshall.

"Thanks," he said to Jan. "You made a faster delivery than I expected. I thought I might have to wait out the afternoon over here."

He looked past Jan to his brother and there was no mockery in his eyes now. He looked on guard, and a little uncertain, as though he was not altogether sure of his younger brother's reception.

"Hi, Pat," he said. "How're you doing?"

Patrick did not hesitate. He scrambled past Jan in such a hurry that he left the boat rocking, with Jan clinging to the seat. In a moment he was on the dock hugging his brother hard with both arms. Jan gave her attention to getting out of the boat. She hated to stand up in anything so wobbly, but there was a ladder nailed to a nearby piling and by holding onto it tightly she managed to clamber up to solid ground.

"Why didn't you write that you were coming home?" Patrick demanded, pounding his brother joyfully on the back.

"I thought I'd better just show up and see how things were," Eddie said. His face, thin and pale above the beard, had lighted over the meeting with his young brother, as Jan had not seen it do before.

Since neither was paying any attention to her, and she

did not want to stay and listen to what was clearly a private conversation, Jan muttered, "Thanks for the ride," though Patrick did not hear, and ran up the embankment and across the road.

The screen door to the veranda was unlocked and Jan went into the house looking for Mrs. Marshall. She found her in the living room packing Jan's things back into her suitcase. The cot Jan had slept on last night had been put away, and the small possessions she had taken out in order to give herself some feeling of being at home had all been put neatly back into the case.

For a moment she stood watching in dismay. Was she to be sent away at once? she wondered. Or was she not to have her things out at all? It was difficult not having a room, or even a private corner of her own.

She studied Mrs. Marshall, wondering how to ask questions. Patrick's mother was probably older than Mom. After all, she had a grown son who was nearly Dad's age. Her hair was turning gray, and although it was neatly combed, there was nothing stylish about it. Her housedress was crisply ironed, but a little old-fashioned, and her shoes were sensible for someone who had to be on her feet a lot. She looked a little like her younger son, except that instead of a scowl, she wore a rather sad expression most of the time. Was that Eddie's fault? Jan wondered.

At last she turned and noticed Jan. "Hello there. Have you had lunch? If not, I'll fix you something right away."

"Gran took me to lunch," Jan said and continued to watch helplessly as her things vanished into the suitcase, each article being neatly folded and put in its place. She wanted to say, "What are you packing everything away for?" but the question might sound rude. If she waited, she would undoubtedly find out.

Mrs. Marshall became suddenly aware of Jan's worried attention. "Oh, dear! I should have told you right away why I'm doing this. There's been a change of plans. I'm not sure your grandmother will approve, but old Mrs. Pendleton isn't one to argue with, so I'm doing what she asks. If your grandmother doesn't think it's a good idea, then we'll just have to move you downstairs again."

"But — but I am downstairs," Jan murmured.

Patrick's mother rubbed the back of her hand across her forehead. "There! You can see how distracted I am. I'm not getting anything straight. Your great-grandmother has decided that you are to have the extra bedroom upstairs. I must say you've made a good impression on her or she wouldn't have you up there for anything. If you'll get your coat and hat from the closet, I'll take you right up. The room is ready for you."

Feeling astonished and more than a little excited, Jan got her things from the hall closet, glancing out of the front door as she did so. Patrick and his brother Eddie were walking arm in arm along the shore road. In a moment they would be out of sight around the bend, and somehow Jan felt relieved as she followed Mrs. Marshall up the stairs. She had a feeling that it would upset Mrs. Marshall all the more to know that Patrick had welcomed the older son home so joyfully.

"Don't make any noise," Mrs. Marshall warned. "Your great-grandmother is napping, as she always does after lunch. I'll take you to your room and you can unpack to suit yourself. I do hope you can manage to be quiet up here and not disturb Mrs. Pendleton. She's too old, I'm afraid, to have a young person so near at hand. But it's her idea and not for me to argue about. Here you are, my dear. There's even a little bathroom you can have for your own."

She pushed open the door of a front room and went inside to pull up blinds that had been drawn against the sun. Jan stood on the threshold watching the splash of sunlight across old-fashioned wallpaper made up of hundreds of tiny, pale pink rosebuds, each with its own miniature leaves and stems. It was like stepping into a sunny garden and Jan could hardly wait for Mrs. Marshall to go away and leave her to enjoy this room which she was, so astonishingly, to have for herself — a room that was to be her very own.

6 THIEF
IN THE NIGHT

THE DAY HAD gone by in a hurry. It was not yet bedtime, but for once Jan was happy to go early to bed. Tonight her room made all the difference. It even made a difference about the lonesomeness for her family that had hovered ready to crush her ever since her arrival. Her loss was a little easier to bear when she did not seem altogether homeless.

The room was in itself a special sort of adventure that invited and comforted her. Not all rooms were like that. Miss Althea's big double living room, for instance, was fascinating to visit—being almost like stepping into a museum because of the interesting things on every hand. But it was not a room Jan could ever feel completely at home in.

On the other hand, this room with the faded rosebud wallpaper, the four-poster bed, the ladder-back rocker that creaked companionably, the little bed table with its reading lamp—this room had spoken to her at once. It was as if it said, "I know you. We belong together. You'll be happy here."

Tonight Gran had given her a tall glass of milk and a plate of gingerbread to bring upstairs. The china plate was painted with tiny violets that seemed to peer out from beneath the plump brown squares. These waited for her on the bed table while she put on her green shorty pajamas that were just right for a warm night. Now she was tucked in, the two big pillows fluffed up behind her, and a book she had found downstairs waiting to be read. She meant to sip milk and eat gingerbread and read as long as she liked, but first she wanted to enjoy her surroundings.

Sunlight had given way to moonlight outdoors and Jan had not drawn the blinds. There was only the dark river out there, and the upper porch beyond her front windows. The side window near her bed overlooked the outer stairway. If anyone came up that stairway tonight — or any night — she would be sure to hear him. And perhaps, for Miss Althea's sake, that was a good thing. What Mr. Chilton had said at the bookstore returned to her mind. He had put into words the feeling on the part of everyone but Miss Althea that such a valuable jade collection should be more carefully guarded.

At least Eddie Marshall was not an outsider, not really a thief sneaking in to loot the house. If he had taken anything last night, it must have been nothing more than that Chinese idol and surely he had some special reason for such an action. Nevertheless, Jan had the feeling that something very strange was going on — something altogether wrong. She wished she knew more about whatever scandal Eddie had been mixed up in. It must have been serious, since it had sent him out of town for a long while.

These thoughts were drawing her from the state of comfort and serenity she had looked forward to, and she put them aside. She reached for her book and sat back to prop it open against her knees. Gran said the books in the case downstairs had belonged to the generations of children who had grown up in this house, and most of them were books about boys. This one was about a girl. It was called *A Little Princess* and it was by a famous author of Gran's generation, Frances Hodgson Burnett. Jan knew that recent editions of this writer's books were in the libraries, but she had never read one of them before.

The gingerbread was light and spicy on her tongue, and it munched up to a pleasantly lasting consistency that she could chew on for quite a while. Milk helped in swallowing and she liked the damp cold feeling of the glass in her hand. Careful now — no spilling.

The story began in a fascinating way:

Once on a dark winter's day, when the yellow fog hung so thick and heavy in the streets of London that the lamps were lighted and the shop windows blazed with gas as they do at night, an odd-looking little girl sat in a cab with her father and was driven rather slowly through the big thoroughfares . . .

Soon Jan was lost in the world of Sara Crewe, who was being parted from her beloved father and put into Miss Minchin's boarding school, where she was not at all happy. Sara was only seven, but her story was so immediately engrossing that Jan did not mind the difference in their age.

So lost was she in her reading that she started at the sound of a knock on her door and returned somewhat mistily from long-ago London town.

"Come in," she called, half expecting Miss Minchin to step right from the pages and come through the door.

Instead, it was Miss Althea who came in. Since Jan had moved upstairs early this afternoon, she had seen little of her great-grandmother. The old lady had been resting much of the time, or had merely nodded to her briefly, showing no inclination to talk. But now, clearly, she had come for a visit. She was still dressed in one of her flowing gowns of Hong Kong silk, but this time the color was a beautiful turquoise—a rich and glowing greenish-blue like the Mystic River early this morning.

As she turned toward a chair Jan noted the twinkle of jade in the tortoiseshell comb that held thick white coils of hair at the back of her head. The old lady sat down carefully with the help of her canes and smiled at her great-granddaughter. Under one arm she had carried a small object wrapped in a handkerchief. She placed this in her lap.

"Don't get out of bed," Miss Althea said. "I'll sit over here and visit for a little while, if you don't mind. You can go back to your book soon."

"Thank you for giving me this room, Miss Althea," Jan murmured, feeling both unexpectedly loving and shy and a little in awe, all at the same moment.

"It's right that you should have it," her great-grandmother said. "Though I had to know what sort of person you were before I could invite you to occupy it. That's why I asked you who you were the moment we met—and I remember your expression! I made up my mind very quickly, once we'd talked a little. You belong in this room."

Jan had felt that herself. She sat very still, waiting for more.

"Eat your gingerbread," Miss Althea said more brusquely. "You can eat and listen at the same time, can't you?"

Thus bidden, Jan broke off a chunk and popped it into her mouth.

"When I was young and came to this house on visits, this room was always mine," the old lady went on. "The house was built by the older Captain Pendleton, Randy's father. Captain Pendleton and my father, Gillespie Osborn, were close friends out in China. The captain always stopped to call on my parents when his ship came through. So when I was sent home after my mother died, I was sometimes permitted to visit here during the summer. This was always my room. The wallpaper has faded and peeled a little, and it is water-stained in places, but I could never bear to replace it. I wanted to keep it the way I remembered because I first met my Randy in this very house. He had a new sailboat in those days and he used to take me out on the river. He even named the boat to please me."

The *Happy Heart*, Jan thought, remembering the model Patrick's grandfather was making for Miss Althea. The sailboat she was talking about, that she had sailed in with Randal Pendleton, must have been the *Happy Heart*. She did not mention its name, however, and Jan did not ask her.

"Later on I married Randy and came to live in this house for good," Miss Althea said. "My sons were born under its roof, and two of them were married here. The eldest to your grandmother. Now that my son is dead, it is her house—I gave it to her long ago. My son was away a lot in the early years of his marriage and at first they had a home elsewhere. But your father used to visit me here when he was a little boy, and he always stayed in this very room. Now you are a part of that same pattern. This is why I say you belong here."

Jan clasped her hands about her knees and looked slowly about the room, savoring what her great-grandmother had told her. It was especially comforting to know

that Dad had slept in this same room, in this very bed—
perhaps when he was exactly the age his daughter was
now.

"If you'll look," Miss Althea said, "you'll find that
Bob carved his initials on the lower left-hand post of the
bed. I spanked him for that, I can assure you. He had
some curious notion about leaving a trail of carved
initials behind wherever he went. I think I persuaded him
from so destructive and conceited a habit. I used to tell
him that if he wanted to make a mark on life, it could
only be done through acts performed, not through scratch-
ing his name on anything."

She smiled at Jan, warmly, proudly.

"Perhaps he listened just a little, because he is making
a mark through his acts—out in Vietnam. But his initials
never came off that bedpost, much as I sandpapered and
polished."

Jan crawled to the foot of the bed and knelt there.
Sure enough, she could make out the markings—small,
rather crooked letters: R.A.P.—Robert Andrew Pendleton. Once "Rap" had been his nickname as a boy. Jan
traced the letters with one finger, her face shining.

"I'm glad I didn't spank him very hard," said Miss
Althea, watching her. "I'm glad the scratches are there
for you to touch."

Never in all her life had Jan found anyone who so
quickly understood what she was thinking and feeling.

"I've brought you something to keep you company
your first night in this room," the old lady said, unwrap-
ping the handkerchief from about the small object it
concealed. She held up the little jade Kwan Yin and Jan
rolled off the bed to come and take it delightedly in her
hand. She looked once more into the lovely, serene face

and found that it cast a quieting spell.

"I'd like to have known the lady the jade carver used for a model," Miss Althea said. "She must have been an intelligent person, kind and very calm. Yet not even this little figure could ever take the place of my Joyful Mountain."

Jan moved the empty gingerbread plate and set the little jade lady on the bed table. It would be comforting to know that she was there during the night, looking so wise and serene.

"You said that once before," Jan said. "You mentioned a Joyful Mountain. What do the words mean?"

"That was the name of a piece of jade. Long ago the master jade carvers of China sometimes carved lumps of jade into what they called 'mountains.' My father was delighted when one of these jade mountains came into his possession. It was carved from a single piece of jade that had the shape of a miniature mountain — perhaps several inches high. There were trees in the jade, a stream and waterfall and craggy rocks. There were houses and men and women as well — nothing standing out by itself, you understand, but all there against the stone in a sort of bas-relief. The scene was such a gay one that the artist named his creation the Joyful Mountain."

"I wish I could have seen it," Jan said.

Miss Althea's deep-set eyes were shadowed with memories. "Where some small children become attached to a stuffed animal or to cuddly dolls, I became devoted to that hard little stone mountain. Not that I was allowed to take it to bed with me! But as soon as I was old enough I read stories into the jade, the way the artist had read pictures. My father and mother used to flatter me by listening to these made-up stories. Once when a wealthy mandarin offered Father a great deal of money for his Joyful Mountain, he refused to sell it. Not only because he was proud to own it, but also because he knew how much I loved it."

"What became of it?" Jan asked.

Slim shoulders, sheathed in turquoise silk, shrugged faintly. "I imagine it is in a museum somewhere in Communist China. It was too large to bring out easily in a handbag, so it wasn't among the small jade pieces my father sent out of the country with me. Then he was caught by the tragedy they called the Boxer rebellion, early in the 1900's. My father died and I never saw him again — or the jade mountain."

Miss Althea looked so sad that Jan tried to change the subject. "Did Gran tell you about talking to Mr. Chilton today?" she asked.

The old lady sighed and returned her attention to the present. "Yes, she did. Mr. Chilton phoned me this afternoon. I haven't decided what I will do as yet. It's true that my jades and porcelains ought to be out in the world giving pleasure to others. Eventually they will go to my children and my children's children. But they are still a gift my father gave me and for my lifetime I want them with me. A loan, perhaps that is different. Not the finer pieces, I think. Not my little Kwan Yin. Possibly some of the porcelains that my father sent home long before the trouble started. Some of the monsters, perhaps. Tomorrow you may help me pick out the pieces we will lend him. Will you do that?"

"I'd love to," Jan said. "What are the monsters?"

Miss Althea reached for her canes and thrust herself slowly to her feet. "You'll see. When I was a small child they used to frighten me. They still do a little. I don't

really like them. You can do my looking for me tomorrow."

"Is the Chinese idol Dad told me about—the one
Eddie took—one of the monsters?"

"There's been altogether too much talk about what is
my business—and Eddie Marshall's," Miss Althea said,
suddenly tart. "But in answer to your question—yes—it
is the very worst monster of all. Not only because it is
ugly, but because it has always annoyed me, mocked me,
bullied me. What's worse, it has always refused to be put
away in a closet with the others. It sits there in the dark
and reproaches me and I always have to bring it out again.
But my life is nearly over and I don't have to listen anymore. It would be good riddance if the old thing has
disappeared forever."

Miss Althea moved toward the door, but Jan could not
let the subject of the idol go, even though it disturbed the
old lady to speak of it.

"Dad said there was a mystery about it. He said he
kept trying to find out something about it when he was a
boy."

Miss Althea paused at the door. "Yes, I remember
that," she said dryly. "He was so energetic in his research that he dropped it on its head one day and took a
chip off one ugly ear. I didn't say so at the time, but I
was always a little sorry he didn't smash it completely
to bits."

"Then why—" Jan began, wondering why her great-
grandmother did not simply break the idol up herself if
she disliked it so much, "—then why—"

Miss Althea had heard enough. "Good night, Janice,"
she said. "Don't worry if you hear me moving about and
turning lights on and off at all hours. Sometimes I do

more sleeping in the daytime than I do at night. We'll talk again in the morning."

Jan hurried to open the door for her. The old lady said a gracious, "Thank you," and returned to her own rooms. When she had gone, Jan yawned widely and stretched to her very fingertips. She was getting sleepy. *A Little Princess* would have to wait until tomorrow. That was the nice thing about a book. It was always there to return to. Movies and television plays were gone so quickly — and most of them were gone for good, but a book was like a constant friend. Even after you'd read it through you could go back and visit with the characters again. Indeed, she had found that a story very often told her more the second and third times she read it. The first time it was the story that held her and she kept reading because she wanted to know what would happen next. The second time she listened more carefully to what the characters were saying and understood their thoughts a good deal better.

Jan looked longingly at the plate that had held gingerbread, but it was decorated only with the blue of its pattern of violets and a few brown crumbs. She dampened a finger on the tip of her tongue and managed to pick up every crumb. Then she tilted the milk glass and waited until a few last drops rolled the long way down the inside of the glass to her lips. It was surprising how hungry she could feel at bedtime. She pushed Kwan Yin a little farther back on the table so she wouldn't fall off, and turned out the lamp.

At first the darkness seemed complete. As her eyes grew used to it she realized how bright with moonlight the night was outdoors. She had a sudden urgent wish to be out in all that glow. Only one of the windows that opened on the porch seemed to have a screen. When she raised the other window as softly as possible, she found she could step through it onto the porch.

Moonlight flooded over her like a shower of gold. She leaned upon the railing and watched the lights of houses on the opposite shore, the lights of a boat on the river. The oak trees and maples whispered their nighttime secrets in a light breeze, but the birds were all asleep.

From somewhere in the house came the shrill ringing of a telephone. The sound seemed to be upstairs and Jan went back inside, wondering who could be calling Miss Althea at this hour. Yes — that was her voice speaking in the other room. The words were blurred, but the tone sounded as if she was angry, perhaps indignant. The conversation lasted only a few moments and then there was a click, followed by silence.

Jan closed the screenless window and locked it, made sure the one with the screen was hooked, and got into bed. For some reason the telephone call and the tone of her great-grandmother's voice made her uneasy. With the lights out she could look through the two curtained windows beside her bed and see the stairs outside. In the daylight there had seemed nothing disturbing about those stairs, in spite of what Neil had told her. Mystic was a small, friendly place. If there were strangers going through because of the Seaport, they were across the river. No one would come over here to this quiet row of captains' houses unless he belonged. Even Eddie Marshall really belonged here. But while everything had seemed cozy and secure in her room when the lights were on, the room now seemed strange to her — unknown, and perhaps not altogether friendly.

By ducking her head she could look under tree branches

and glimpse the house where the Kents lived only a short distance away. Over there lights burned downstairs, and there was a single light in an upstairs bedroom. Probably that was Neil's room.

She yawned again and wriggled down under the sheet to think more comfortably about her day. For quite a while, she realized dreamily, she had not been homesick at all. This room and her great-grandmother's visit had been so interesting that the aching had been forgotten. The minute she thought of her family, the hurt came back full force. Fortunately, she was too sleepy to enjoy her suffering. Her lids drooped — and that was all she remembered until some time after midnight.

She knew it was after midnight because the grandfather's clock downstairs had wakened her and started her counting on the first chime. She had marked the chimes all the way to twelve and then gone back to sleep. The next time she wakened it was not the clock that summoned her to consciousness, but something far more chilling.

Lightly, though clearly, the sound came — and at once she was wide awake. It was the stealthy sound of footsteps on the stairs outside her windows. She rolled over in bed so that her head came barely above one windowsill, and peered out from behind crossed curtains.

A dark figure was coming softly up the outside stairs. The moonlight had shifted and the stairs were not as bright as they had been, but she could not mistake so large a moving shadow. She lay down in bed at once, shivering with alarm. The old steps creaked no matter how quietly the intruder moved. At the top step she heard the door opening, very softly, very secretly, as he let himself into the porch. Why had that door been left open? she wondered. Didn't Miss Althea lock up before she went to bed?

Jan lay flat on her back with her heart thumping so loudly that she could hardly tell which was heart and which were the outside sounds of someone who might be a thief in the night.

7 THE BEGINNING OF TROUBLE

SHE COULD NOT lie here in fright while someone came secretly into her great-grandmother's house, Jan told herself. In spite of her shivering, she crept out of bed and padded in bare feet to the front windows and looked through onto the porch. Inside, the darkness hid her, but moonlight still touched the porch.

The man was there and she saw that he carried something large and bulky in his arms. Was this the object Neil had described? He tiptoed across the porch to Miss Althea's front door, held his bundle in one arm, and reached for the knob.

She must do something, Jan thought. She must get through to the other part of the house without rousing or frightening the old lady and confront Eddie Marshall. It was not as if this were some unknown intruder of whom she need be afraid. She went quickly to the door that opened into Miss Althea's living room and pushed it ajar just a crack.

Through the narrow slit light flooding from lamps blinded her for an instant. She blinked hard to escape the sudden dazzle and saw that Miss Althea stood there in the center of the room as if she awaited the intruder. She held herself determinedly erect between her canes, the flowing turquoise of her gown melting into the wheat-gold carpet beneath her feet. Behind her head the red lacquer of a tray on the wall made a frame for her white hair. She faced the porch door, and when Jan opened the crack a little more she saw that Eddie Marshall had come through the door and stood facing the old lady, holding in his arms what must surely be the Chinese idol.

"Good evening, Eddie," Miss Althea said quietly. "I'm glad you phoned me that you were coming this time. Why did you take my old enemy away in the first place? And why have you brought him back?"

She ought not listen, Jan thought. This was a conversation not meant for her. Yet while they spoke of the idol she had to listen. She had to learn all she could.

Eddie came farther into the room, closing the door behind him. He went to a teakwood table and set his burden down carefully. He stood before it and Jan could not glimpse the figure through the narrow crack.

"You wouldn't listen to me," Eddie said. "You told me you wouldn't bother with me anymore. You sent me away."

"I'm too old to become involved in other people's troubles," Miss Althea said. "I only want to be left alone."

"That's why I took the old fellow with me when I left," Eddie said. "As long as I had him, I knew you'd have to see me again to let me bring him back. You'd have to listen."

"You could have dropped him in the river, for all I care!" The old lady's voice had risen a little, as though he had thrust past her guard.

Eddie's soft laughter was not pleasant to hear. "Oh,

I'd never do that. Don't you remember that Bob Pendleton and I always thought there was something peculiar about Old Fang-Tooth? Though you sure made it hard for us to get at him when we were young."

"I hardly needed your help," Miss Althea said. "Don't you suppose I had found out long ago all he had to tell me?"

"I suppose so," Eddie said. "Anyway, I didn't discover anything new. If I'd had time, I might have taken him to someone who knows about such things, to find out if he's more valuable than you think."

"In which case I suppose you'd have sold him and been off about your business? Perhaps that is what you should have done, instead of coming back here to make your entire family unhappy."

Eddie whirled angrily away and took a turn about the room, coming so close to Jan's door that she barely closed the crack in time. After that she stood with her ear pressed against the door panel, trying to hear. Eddie frightened her. She was no longer confident that he meant her great-grandmother no harm.

Outdoors, wind rustled the trees, and the sound came through her open windows so that she could not hear a thing from Miss Althea's living room. Holding her breath, she drew the door open once more the thinnest of cracks.

Miss Althea was sitting down — which must mean that she wasn't afraid of Eddie. In fact, she was telling him to sit down and stop stamping around. Jan heard the creak of a chair across the room out of sight.

"Patrick came to see me this afternoon," the old lady said. "He pleaded for you in a way you hardly deserve. Even if you hadn't brought this old fellow back, I suppose I should have had to see you again."

"Good for Pat!" Eddie said.

"Be quiet and listen to me," Miss Althea told him sternly. "What we are going to talk about will be private — something between you and me alone. I do not want you running about telling people how soft I am and how you could always get around me. But first I'd like to speak to my great-granddaughter. You may close your door at once, Janice. I did not invite you to occupy my guest room so that you could spy upon me or listen to private conversations. We will speak further about this in the morning."

Jan closed the door quickly, engulfed by embarrassment, guilt, and dismay. She fled back to her bed and hid her shame beneath the covers. From the living room she could hear the ring of Eddie Marshall's laughter and she disliked him all the more intensely for laughing.

She knew very well that she should not have been listening, but curiosity had got the better of her. Now she had disgraced herself and angered her great-grandmother — which was not a very good start if she meant to stay out of trouble this summer. Painfully she remembered what Miss Althea had said about their being friends. Perhaps that was spoiled entirely. And it was all her own fault for doing what she knew she should not do.

For a long time she lay listening miserably to night whisperings outside and the sounds of the river. After a while her feeling of embarrassment subsided a little and curiosity once more took its place. She tried to sort out the meaning of what she had heard, but since she lacked the key to the puzzle, nothing made much sense. Yet Eddie Marshall, too, believed there was some mystery about the Chinese idol, just as her father had, and the desire to examine it firsthand began to grow in Jan to an alarming degree. Alarming because she was already in trouble and because she remembered her mother's warning not to indulge any of those "wild ideas" that so often led her to disaster. She must be very, very careful.

Having thus admonished herself, she gave her thoughts over to the mystery of the Chinese idol that her father had called Old Fang-Tooth. So far, she realized, she had not even learned how the idol had come into Miss Althea's hands. Dad had backed so hastily away from the subject—leaving her tantalized—that she had very little information to go on. She did not know why everyone seemed to think there was a mystery about it. This she must somehow take steps to discover for herself. Very safe steps, of course—nothing that would upset Miss Althea further.

In the next room the murmur of voices went on, the words inaudible. At last the sound lulled Jan back to sleep and this time she slumbered so deeply that she did not hear Eddie Marshall when he left the house and went down the outside stairs to disappear into the night. She did not know when the old lady went to bed. In the morning she overslept and awoke to bright sunshine and a sense of concern and urgency.

The concern was because her great-grandmother was angry with her, and the urgency because her curiosity about the idol was still so great. As she washed and dressed she began to wish for someone to talk to about all that had happened. She would not dare to tell Gran, lest permission to occupy this room be canceled because she had disturbed Miss Althea. Could she talk to Neil? she wondered. How far could he be trusted to keep quiet about anything she might tell him? And how good would his reasoning be on any of this? She realized that she did not really know him at all. If only Dorothy were here!

When she left her room to come downstairs, Jan took the little jade figure of Kwan Yin with her and replaced it on the table near the window. Then she looked quickly down the long expanse of her great-grandmother's double parlor. Miss Althea was there. She lay back in her big armchair, with her feet on an ottoman, napping gently. She wore a dull, gray dress this morning and she looked old and frail with her eyes closed, the intelligence that usually lighted her face hidden behind their shutters.

Jan tiptoed fearfully across the pale-gold carpet so she could see the high corner ledge at the back of the room. Sure enough, it had an occupant this morning. A squat, green ceramic figure about a foot high sat upon the shelf. She could see its hunched shoulders and the folds of a green robe, with some sort of yellow cord about its fat middle. The figure had been set with its face to the wall and she could not tell what the front of it looked like.

Her fingers tingled with the desire to touch it, to take it down, but she did not dare, with Miss Althea right there in the room. She was already in quite enough trouble as it was.

She fled the room before temptation overcame her and hurried downstairs. Gran was finishing breakfast and talking earnestly to Mrs. Marshall. Both women said, "Good morning," somewhat absently to Jan, and Gran motioned her to her place at the table. Then she went right on talking to Patrick's mother.

"Mrs. Pendleton has made this decision," she said. "She decided yesterday afternoon after Patrick came to see her. And you know there's no changing her mind once she gets a notion firmly lodged. I'm worried, and I know you are too, but I think we must give this a try.

Perhaps it will all work out for the best."

Mrs. Marshall dipped slices of bread into egg and milk and dropped them into sizzling butter to make French toast for Jan. She spoke with her back turned, her voice sounding tired and subdued.

"I don't know what to do. I really don't. Old Mrs. Pendleton has a good heart and she was always as fond of the boy when he was young as though he had been her own grandson. She wants to help him, and I'm very grateful. Though what his father will say, I don't know. My husband has never forgiven Eddie."

Gran smiled at her old friend affectionately. "We must certainly give him another chance, now that he has come home. We can't condemn him without offering him that chance. Mother is right."

Mrs. Marshall nodded soberly as she turned the French toast over with a spatula. "Your breakfast will be ready in a minute, Janice," she said. "Pour yourself some milk from the refrigerator, there's a good girl."

Jan sprang up to help and when she sat down again with the glass of cold milk beside her plate, Gran was looking at her.

"I hope you slept well last night. How is your room?"

"I love it," Jan said fervently, avoiding the question about sleeping well. "Miss Althea and I had a lovely visit last night." She did not mention that everything was much less lovely later on.

"That's fine," Gran said. "Mother has taken an interest in you and that makes me happy. She needs a new interest in her life. But it must not be a disturbing interest. I'm sure you understand that."

Jan fixed her attention on the French toast and bacon Mrs. Marshall had set before her and said nothing.

"What are you going to do today?" Gran asked, pushing her chair back from the table. "Any plans?"

"I'm not sure yet," Jan said. "Perhaps I'll come over to the Seaport later. There are some things I'd like to do around here first."

"That's fine. I have to run along." Gran picked up her handbag from a chair and took out the car keys, adding, as if it were an afterthought, "Mrs. Marshall's older son Eddie is working for us today. After you delivered his note to Patrick and Patrick talked to Mother, we had a little consultation. There's always a lot of work around a house and yard that is too much for women to handle. Eddie is going to help us out for a while."

Because Miss Althea had insisted on it, Jan thought. This must have been what she was talking to Eddie about last night. Gran still seemed worried, however, and she exchanged a thoughtful look with Mrs. Marshall as she went out the back door.

For the moment Jan gave her main attention to French toast spread with butter and flooded with maple syrup. Now and then as she ate she stole a quick glance at Mrs. Marshall. The housekeeper's eyes weren't red this morning, but she continued to look sad and concerned. More than once she went to the back door and looked outside. Jan could hear the sound of a lawn mower, so Eddie must already be at work. What was it he had done to disturb everyone so much? she wondered for the dozenth time.

She finished breakfast and went out upon the front porch to find that he had moved around to the front of the house. When she appeared he was leaning on the handle of the lawn mower and mopping sweat from his forehead. This morning the thin face above the beard looked a little less pale, as though being outdoors was already doing him good.

He saw Jan and grinned at her. "You were a good kid to get that note to Pat. As you can see, he has landed me a job. Thanks to the old lady upstairs."

Jan went slowly down the steps and sauntered toward him speculatively.

He went on speaking, as though her silent watching made him uneasy. "I knew Pat wouldn't let me down — even if I am the family black sheep."

Jan decided on a bold question. If no one else would tell her, perhaps Eddie himself would explain. "How did you happen to turn into a black sheep?" she asked, coming to a stop directly in front of him.

At once his friendliness vanished. "That's none of your business, is it?" he growled and turned back to the lawn mower. It whirred furiously as he rolled it across the scant, weedy grass of the front lawn.

Jan left the front yard and walked along the road toward the Kents' house, looking for Neil. She was just in time to meet him as he wheeled his bike toward the road. When he saw her he changed his mind about riding away and leaned the bicycle against a tree, beckoning to her urgently.

"Were you going somewhere?" Jan asked as she joined him.

He shook his blond head, his eyes alive with a suppressed excitement that made them seem bluer than ever. "I was going to ride around. I'd rather talk to you."

She felt pleased. He was a very good-looking boy, and although he wasn't always friendly, he was nicer than Patrick Marshall. And he looked a lot cleaner and neater than Patrick. This morning he wore dungarees, but they were as clean as his starched blue shirt.

She followed as Neil led the way around to the side yard of his house, out of sight of the Pendletons'. The moment they reached this shaded side, he fairly pounced upon her.

"Does your grandmother know what sort of man she's got working for her? Does she know he's a convict?"

Jan gasped. So this was the secret. This was why everyone was behaving in such an uneasy fashion about Eddie Marshall.

"*I* didn't know," she admitted. "Who told you?"

Neil's strange excitement seemed to increase. Boredom had left him and he was eager to impart his information.

"A man from town came to see Dad before he left the house this morning. When he saw that fellow out in your backyard, his eyes practically popped and he said, 'I didn't know he was out of jail.' I hung around listening and I heard him tell Dad that this fellow was arrested in connection with a holdup in New York City. He was convicted and sent to prison. The man said he didn't like to see him working around a house with only women in it because he was a no-good and a dangerous character."

For some reason, shocked though she was, Jan had an impulse to protect and defend, not Eddie Marshall — she didn't care about him — but Gran and Miss Althea, who knew all about Eddie and were trying to give him another chance.

"He's Mrs. Marshall's son," she told Neil. "And I don't think he's going to be dangerous around a place where his mother works. He came to see my great-grandmother again last night and she had a talk with him. I guess he needs work and she wants to help him."

Neil's blue eyes widened. "You mean he was only going to visit your great-grandmother night before last when I saw him on the stairs in the rain?"

"Of course," Jan said lightly.

"And he wasn't stealing anything?"

"Not stealing," said Jan. "That was just an old Chinese idol he borrowed. Something Miss Althea says isn't valuable, though there's some sort of mystery about it. I don't know why he took it, but he brought it back last night when he had another talk with my great-grandmother."

Neil was listening so intently that she felt a little flattered. She had not known she could be so interesting.

"That's something about the old idol!" he said. "What's the whole story?"

"I don't really know," Jan said. "My great-grandmother doesn't like to talk about it."

Neil considered this. "It's pretty odd that this fellow would take the idol and then bring it back. I'd like to know more about this."

So would she, Jan thought. In spite of being pleased by his interest, she had a feeling that she should not be discussing all this with Neil.

"I've never seen a convict before," Neil said, sounding excited again. "Not in real life." He moved to the corner of the house and peered cautiously around at Eddie Marshall and the lawn mower. "Maybe you could fix it so I could meet him?"

His words made Jan regret having told Neil anything. They made her feel a little squirmy. She did not like Eddie Marshall, but neither did she think it fair for Neil to act as though he were some sort of—of animal in a zoo. Something on exhibit.

"Maybe it's kinder to let him alone," she said. "Probably there'll be all sorts of people staring at him and whispering behind his back."

"Why shouldn't there be?" Neil asked. "I'd think he wouldn't have the nerve to show his face around here again. Do you know why he came back?"

Jan had already wondered about that. She had the uneasy feeling that it might be because of what Eddie thought he could get out of a very old lady like Althea Pendleton. But she wasn't going to say this to Neil.

"I haven't any idea," she told him.

Neil seemed to have forgotten his own question. He was shaking his head darkly, wrinkling up his blond eyebrows as a new thought occurred to him. "What do you know? Bossy, important old Patrick Marshall has a brother who's been in prison! Maybe I can have some fun with this after all."

Jan had heard enough. "I think that's a dreadful thing to say!" she cried. Her indignation was rising again. She had never known two more annoying boys than Neil Kent and Patrick Marshall. Both of them were impossible and if she was going to find a friend in this place, she would certainly have to look somewhere else. Eddie undoubtedly deserved all the mean things anyone could say about him, but if he really meant to turn over a new leaf, he would never have a chance if people acted like this.

Neil noted her indignation. "Hey, wait a minute! Don't get mad so fast. You don't get what I mean."

"I thought I did," Jan snapped.

Neil was smiling now. Not laughing at her — but smiling in a friendly sort of way. "If you'll stop throwing off sparks, there's something I'd like to show you," he said. "It's sort of a hobby of mine. Though maybe a little more than that because I'm doing it for a reason. If you want to, you can help me on it. I don't mean just introducing me to your yardman. There's someone a whole lot more interesting you could help me to meet. Come on inside and I'll show you what I mean."

When he behaved like this, she was ready to do as he asked, though his changes of mood confused her a little. At least Patrick Marshall was all of one piece and always the same. He was unpleasant all the time.

They went in by a side door. The radio was on very loud in the living room and Neil's mother was running a vacuum cleaner at the same time. Her blond hair was pinned up in huge pink rollers all over her head and her face was shiny with cream. She was wearing a shift that was completely shapeless and printed all over in large green and yellow flowers. When Neil brought Jan into the room, she turned off the vacuum and talked above the radio.

"I told you to stay outside until I got the cleaning done. If I can't even get cleaning help in this one-horse town, you can at least keep out from underfoot while I'm working."

Jan had said, "Hello," without being answered and she wished uncomfortably that she were somewhere else. She turned toward the door, but Neil reached out and caught her by the arm.

"Oh, Mom!" he said. "Don't be like that. Leave the old carpet and I'll finish it for you later. I want to show Jan my tape recorder. She's going to help me."

His mother relented and gave him an unhappy smile. "O.K., kids. Go ahead. I need a rest anyway. Close the door, will you? All that talking gives me a headache."

Mystified, Jan followed Neil across the living room to the door of what was apparently a closed-in sun porch.

"Come on," said Neil impatiently and gave Jan a little shove that sent her into the middle of the sun porch. There she stood looking around in considerable surprise. Whatever she had expected, it was not this.

8 NEIL'S HOBBY

THERE WERE NO curtains on the sun porch windows, but there were blinds which could be drawn if the sun became too bright. A rather scuffed straw rug covered part of the floor, and on a round table stood a portable tape recorder. The top was open and there was a tape in place, ready to be played. The recorder's microphone was plugged in and lying on the table. There were a couple of battered yard chairs in the room, made of aluminum tubing, with green plastic cushions. Against a wall near the door was the one new piece of furniture — a maple desk piled with flat tape boxes, tangled strands of old tape, books, letters, ball-point pens. Some of the drawers were half open, showing their tumbled contents.

Neil looked about with proprietary pride, as if none of the confusion mattered. "This is my studio," he said.

Jan stepped closer to the desk. On the wall above it photographs and snapshots had been pasted with the help of cellophane tape. Many of them appeared to be autographed to Neil. Though she studied face after face, however, and made out some of the signatures, she did not find a face or a name that she recognized.

"Who are they?" she asked hesitantly, hoping she would not offend this rather touchy boy by her ignorance.

"Oh, you wouldn't know any of those people," he said. "They aren't famous or anything. They're people I've interviewed. I'll put all the tapes I've made in order in my file when I have time to get organized."

Jan regarded him with new interest. "You mean you do interviews and have them broadcast?"

"Not broadcast, silly! Not yet, anyway. Interviewing people is only my hobby right now."

It seemed a strange hobby. Jan peered at a photograph of a man dressed in overalls sitting on a flight of cement steps.

"That was our janitor back in New York," Neil said. "Of course I didn't use him because he was a janitor—though that might be interesting too, in some ways. During World War II he was a prisoner in Germany and he gave me a real good interview."

"But—but why?" Jan asked blankly. "Why do you collect interviews?"

"Sit down and I'll tell you about it," Neil said, cheerful enough now that he was in his own element. "My Uncle Hank is in radio. He's an announcer and he doesn't care about doing interviews. He wants to have his own news program someday. Lots of times he has taken me to the studio and let me watch programs from the control room. That's how I got this idea about being a radio interviewer when I grow up. Uncle Hank says there's no time like now for getting started. Christmas before last he bought me that tape recorder and told me to get going. He said I didn't need to talk to famous people, but to anyone who'd had interesting experiences or worked at something interesting. He said it would be good practice for me—learning what questions to ask and how to get people to talk."

Jan looked with more interest at the pictures on the wall. "I think that's wonderful," she said warmly. "And it must be fun too."

Neil nodded, pleased with her approval. "Mom thinks I'm nuts, and Dad thinks it's a waste of time when I can go into his business if I want when I grow up. But some of the talks have turned out so well that my teachers at school have had me play them in class. When the time comes and I'm old enough to get a job, Uncle Hank says I'll be ready to do small jobs in radio and then work up to being an interviewer. I can keep it going when I get to college. Maybe I'll even be famous by that time. A paper out on Long Island wrote me up and printed my picture last year."

This was all quite fascinating, Jan thought. She liked Neil better now that she knew about this hobby. Talking about it, he no longer seemed such a bored and listless person. What was more, she could better understand his interest in Eddie Marshall.

"It's your great-grandmother I'd like to talk to." Neil broke in on her thoughts. "Eddie too — though I think it would be pretty hard to get him to talk. But Mrs. Pendleton has had a pretty interesting life — escaping from China when her father was killed, and all that. If she's still got all her marbles and — "

"She is a very smart woman," Jan said quickly. "I don't think she would want to have her words recorded, though. She has sort of — well, sort of retired."

"You could ask her for me, couldn't you?" Neil said. "If I can talk to her, I'll bet I can persuade her. Old ladies usually like me. I'm such a sweet, charming little boy, you know." He made a silly face at Jan, looking cross-eyed.

She had to laugh, though a bit ruefully. She suspected

that Neil could put on quite an act of being flattering and charming when he chose. In fact, that was what he was doing with her, trying to win her over so she would intercede with Miss Althea for him.

"I don't want to ask her," Jan said. "I can't bother her like that."

Neil looked crestfallen, but he did not give up. "How do you know this wouldn't be an interesting thing for her to do? Why is it up to you to say what she does or doesn't want? Maybe she should decide for herself."

This was putting it in a new light. Maybe it would be interesting, after all. Perhaps Miss Althea should have a chance to refuse or accept for herself. How could anyone be absolutely sure about what so surprising a person as Miss Althea would like to do?

"All right, I'll ask her," she promised Neil, and tried to quiet her own immediate qualms over the thought of asking for this interview. Miss Althea was still displeased with her, and they had not yet had that talk about what happened last night.

Neil's mother came to the door. "The housekeeper has phoned from your house," she said to Janice. "Your great-grandmother wants you whenever you can come up to see her."

Jan stood up, her concern increasing. "I'll go right away. She wants me to help pick out some of her jade collection for an exhibit at the Seaport museum." She could only hope it was that.

"The Chinese treasure?" Neil asked, his eyes lighting.

This time it was Jan who laughed. "You can ask her about it if you get a chance to interview her," she said as she followed Neil's mother to the door.

As she ran across to the other house she felt both re-

luctant and curious at the same time. Her great-grandmother was sitting in her armchair waiting for her when
Jan entered the room.

"I'm glad you came right away," she said. "Mr. Chilton will be over later to pick up whatever I decide to lend
him for the exhibit. So we have work to do. Will you
help me?"

"Of course, Miss Althea," Jan said, almost breathless
with relief. Perhaps her great-grandmother meant to say
nothing about last night, after all.

"We'll begin with the porcelain monsters," the old
lady directed. "That big carved cabinet is locked, but
you have only to turn the key to open the doors. I always
have the feeling that it's safer if the key is turned. I don't
really see how they could get it open from the inside."

Jan smiled. She understood this sort of fantasy. Miss
Althea was joking, yet not exactly joking. She knew
there were more things in the world that could not be
fully understood than grown-ups sometimes admitted.
It was pleasantly frightening to think of a lot of squirmy
porcelain monsters shut up in there, wishing they could
get out and probably fighting with one another.

"I'll open the door carefully," she promised, and her
great-grandmother nodded without smiling.

As Jan knelt before the big carved door of the cabinet,
she flung a quick look over her shoulder toward a high
corner of the room. The Chief Monster was still there in
his place — Old Fang-Tooth — his back to her, staring at
the wall. How was she ever going to get him down when
Miss Althea was nearly always right at hand in this very
room?

She reached for the cabinet key. It was slightly stub-
born, but after opposing her for a moment, it squeaked

in the lock and Jan pulled the double doors open a crack. Inside all was dark and silent, as though the ugly, crawly things had glimpsed the daylight and were sitting utterly still, ready to fly out in her face the moment she gave them a chance. She had a sudden ridiculous impulse to slam the doors shut and turn the key.

"You can open them all the way," Miss Althea said. "The light of day is always alarming to wickedness. They're afraid of us now."

Jan smiled again, accepting the half-serious game. She pulled the double doors wide open and a wave of stale incense rushed out, but that was all. She could see them in there — the ugly creatures — and she reached in and drew one out.

It was a strange-looking lion-dog, indeed a monstrous thing, and oddly beautiful at the same time. The blue and gold and red colors were lovely, and every curl of its thick mane was gracefully wrought in the porcelain. But its round eyes stared at her venomously and its teeth looked dangerously sharp.

"Ugh!" Jan said and placed it on the floor.

"That's Hugo," Miss Althea said. "They all have names because I named them when I was about six years old. I thought they would behave better if I could call each one by an English name."

The next creature was a dragon named Sophie and this one Jan put in a place apart. For all her undulating tail and green scales, her flared nostrils that must be spouting fire, and her long spiked tongue, she was a handsome demon and surely deserved to be put on exhibit if Mr. Chilton wanted her.

So they went through the collection, one by one. The handsomest piece of all was a panther — completely black and glossy, from his twitching tail to the tip of his sniffing nose, except for two green eyes that seemed to glare at Jan out of the black face.

"That's Rudolpho, the guardian of a tomb," Miss Althea said. "His job was to keep evil spirits away from the dead. I thought he ought to have a distinguished name."

Jan stroked Rudolpho's glossy back. "Then he's a good monster, after all." Her great-grandmother seemed so relaxed and friendly that Jan decided to risk something. "Are you going to let Mr. Chilton take the one up there?" She nodded in the direction of the high shelf.

Miss Althea's white head moved in a quick negative gesture and she frowned. "Certainly not. He doesn't belong with these good things — he's too crude and ugly."

"How did he come to you?" Jan asked, holding her breath lest the old lady once more shy away from the subject of the idol. But for once she did not.

"He was given to my father when I was quite young — by a Chinese friend who made the figure and presented him to Father as a piece of his own work. The craftsmanship was very crude, but Father kept the old fellow out of sentiment, because of his friend. When trouble came and I had left the house, Father sent him to me by a Chinese servant to the family that was protecting me. I've been dutiful about keeping it with me ever since, even though I've sometimes been annoyed with the thing when it tries to blame me or reproach me."

This was puzzling. How, Jan wondered, could the idol give blame or reproach? She dared not ask too many questions, lest the old lady cease to talk about it entirely.

Her great-grandmother's gaze had traveled above

Jan's head to rest on the green expanse of the idol's back, but she did not look annoyed at the moment. Her eyes had softened and she was smiling a rather wistful smile, as though she was amused by some secret joke.

Jan dared one more question. "Why must it face the wall all the time?"

Her great-grandmother returned to the present abruptly. "You would understand if you saw its face. It's not something I want to have watching me day in and day out. Never mind that old thing. If you think we've made the best possible selection of porcelains for Mr. Chilton, there are a few little horrors among the jade pieces that we might lend him too. Put back the discards, Janice, and we'll have a look at the jades."

Jan did as she was told and then opened the glass cabinet where the jade was kept.

"We'll begin with the Five Poisons," Miss Althea directed. I can remember a painting Father had of Chang Tao-ling, who was a famous alchemist born nearly two thousand years ago. In the picture he was seated on the back of a tiger, with its foot crushing those five dreadful creatures that make the poisons. They are used for medicinal purposes in China, of course, but they are also dangerous to man. Look for an amulet of white jade carved with a lot of open work. You'll recognize the poisonous creatures — the spider, the centipede, the toad, the snake, and the lizard."

Jan found the eerie little piece with its open carving, the spider clearly evident with its crawly legs, the snake's body making a graceful coil opposite the curve of the lizard.

After that she picked out a little jade fox — an ominous animal in all Oriental literature, Miss Althea said, be-

cause it was often seen coming out of graveyards and the Chinese believed it embodied the souls of the dead.

When everything was ready, Miss Althea gave a sigh of satisfaction. "Good! You've helped me wonderfully, Janice. I think Mr. Chilton will be pleased. Of course I won't lend him my Kwan Yin, even though he has always looked at her longingly. I know he considers her the most valuable and most artistic piece in the collection. But she doesn't belong among the monsters. Now I'm tired, child. I'm going into my bedroom and lie down for a while. Will you stay here and guard my treasures until Mr. Chilton comes?"

It took all Jan's strength of will to keep her immediate thought from showing in her face, to keep her gaze from darting toward that corner shelf. She fixed her eyes on her great-grandmother's face as the old lady struggled to her feet with the help of her ivory-headed canes. As she watched the old lady move in her slow, painful way across the room, she forgot the idol because of the ache of pity in her throat. She longed to do something to help. She could understand how her father—who remembered Miss Althea in her stronger, younger days—must have felt seeing her like this.

"Stop feeling sorry for me!" Miss Althea said sharply. As she reached her bedroom door, she eased herself about on her canes and regarded her great-granddaughter severely. "Pity is something I won't have. Your father was dripping with it when he was here recently and it irritated me terribly."

"He was only sorry because you seemed to—to be giving up and turning into a—a—" Jan broke off.

"A vegetable. I know. I haven't gone that far yet. I'm still able to decide what I want out of life, and by this time I have a right to avoid the unpleasant."

Jan was silent, thinking of Eddie Marshall working at his lawn mower because Miss Althea had given him a job. She hoped with all her heart that nothing unpleasant would ever again touch this very old lady.

Miss Althea went into the bedroom and closed the door behind her with a little snap that was like an exclamation mark set after her words. Jan sat very still, listening to the sound of shades being drawn in the other room, of bedsprings creaking, and the sound of a cane as it fell to the floor. For at least five minutes she sat in silence, with the monsters on the floor all around her. Then she got softly to her feet, barely missing the Five Poisons — and made her way across the room toward the one far corner that held her interest. This might be the only chance she would have in a long while.

She had to take it.

9 OLD FANG-TOOTH

THERE WAS NOTHING nearby that she could stand on to reach the shelf and she brought a straight chair very quietly from the small kitchen at the rear of the apartment. She made no sound as she placed it on a corner of the rug and climbed upon it.

She could just reach the idol and she found that her breath was coming fast as she placed her two hands cautiously about the squat body, testing its weight. It was fairly heavy, but she could lift it from the shelf without any trouble. Holding it carefully, she stepped down from the chair. Once she had the thing in her hands, she was not at all sure what to do with it. If her great-grandmother changed her mind suddenly about resting and came into the room, there would never be time to get the idol back on its shelf. So she might just as well be caught fully as to be caught halfway.

She carried the image to the front windows and set it down beside the little jade figure of Kwan Yin. The black-and-gold lacquer table was low and Jan seated herself on the floor so that her eye level came about even with the Chief Monster. In spite of the fact that she was prepared for something enormously ugly and menacing, she gasped as she looked into its dreadful face, and a shiver of fear ran through her.

Although the robes the thing wore were the garb of a Chinese gentleman, the face was horribly inhuman. The eyes were completely round, with black eyeballs starting wildly from the circling white. The nose was flat, and there were no lips to the mouth, but merely a wide red gash from which ugly fangs jutted. The head was mostly bald, with straight-up tufts of black hair on each side above pointed animal ears. It was a face to dream about in nightmares, and after staring at it in stunned silence for a moment, Jan covered her face with her hands and tried to blink away the horrid vision. When she opened her eyes and looked again, the horror was still there. No wonder Miss Althea kept it in a dark corner with its face turned to the wall. No wonder they called it Old Fang-Tooth.

Jan swallowed a few times and forced herself to examine the crudely made china figure more carefully. Why on earth would Gillespie Osborn's Chinese friend give him such a thing? Or make anything like it in the first place? The porcelain monsters were dreadful too, but they were works of art. Why had Miss Althea's father saved this when far more valuable things were lost?

Jan turned the figure around and found that she could think better if she looked at its back. Nothing about it told her a single thing. Without looking, but just feeling with her fingertips, she prodded its eyes and ears and snarling mouth. She even tapped the flat little nose, but there were no openings through to the interior. When she lifted it in both hands and gave it a good shake, nothing rattled inside. Whatever secret there might be — if there was a secret — must lie on the outside of the image.

She laid it on its side and examined the base. The figure sat with crossed legs beneath its green robe, forming a flat base to rest upon. Over the base had been glued a piece of woven matting, so the figure would not scratch any polished surface upon which it might be placed. A corner of this matting was loose and Jan found that she could turn it back a little way to display the rough, unfinished clay beneath.

There seemed to be some sort of marking in the base. Perhaps the artist had set the Chinese characters of his name into the clay before it dried. Jan turned the figure toward the light and bent to examine the irregular marks, and as she did so a prickle ran up the back of her neck. Eagerly she tried to push the glued matting back a little further, but it resisted her fingers. These weren't Chinese characters at all. They were English letters that formed two words!

Jan traced the lettering again with one finger and read the words softly aloud: "For Rose"—that was all that could be read. If there was anything more, it was hidden beneath the firmly glued matting. Jan scratched at the straw with one finger, but it would not come loose and she dared not rip the rest of it off, much as she would have liked to.

She sat back on her heels and regarded the ugly thing with a pleasure and excitement she had never expected to feel about it. All these years the mystery had been hidden—until now, when it had come to light for Janice Pendleton. While Eddie was carrying the image up and down the stairs he must have loosened a corner of the matting to reveal the words. It had been for her—for the great-great-granddaughter of Gillespie Osborn, to discover that a message of some sort seemed to have been scratched into the rough clay base of the idol.

Who could Rose have been? And why was this piece *for* her? Here was mystery indeed. And it was mystery she could not very well solve without Miss Althea's help. Her great-grandmother would have to know about this. They would strip off the matting together and read the rest of the message — if there was a message.

Jan no longer worried about being discovered examining the ugly figure. She had something real to report that justified her taking the image down from its shelf. She had just reached out to turn back the matting corner once more and reread the two puzzling words when the porch door opened suddenly and a man strode into the room. It was Eddie Marshall. Jan gasped and took her hand abruptly from the figure.

"Oops!" he said, mocking her as usual. "I scared you, didn't I?" His eyes had lighted at once upon the image lying on its side and he laughed softly. "You've got a guilty conscience, haven't you? After all that eavesdropping last night — now this! Pretty sneaky, aren't you?"

More than ever Jan felt that she disliked this man — no matter whether her great-grandmother wanted to help him or not. She had a strong feeling that he was taking advantage of the old lady and that it was her duty to protect Miss Althea in any way possible.

"You startled me," she explained with as much dignity as she could summon, "because I didn't expect anyone to walk in without knocking or ringing the bell. My great-grandmother is resting. You can't see her now."

"I don't want to see her," he said. "I don't have to ring bells to come in. Mrs. Pendleton has given me a place to sleep up in the tower room. That's where I'm going. If you don't mind, Miss Janice Pendleton."

He started across the room, leaving her astonished, only to pause as he came opposite the collection of monsters and jade that had been set out to await Mr. Chilton's inspection.

"Well, will you look at this!" he said, and dropped to one knee to examine the display. "I haven't had a glimpse of these fellows since I was a kid. How come they're spread out on the floor here? Have you been sneaking things from the cabinets behind Great-granny's back?"

Jan was so indignant she merely glared at him, unable to find words.

"Seems to me I remember a small jade goddess that belongs to the collection," he went on. "Where is she?"

Jan had no wish to answer that, but Eddie's glance, traveling the room, fell once more upon the Chinese idol and found Kwan Yin on the table beyond.

"So there she is!" he said, and came to pick up the little jade lady. "The goddess of mercy! Guess I don't believe in her. But she's worth a pile of dough, this one."

Jan fumed, but there was nothing she could say or do. How could Miss Althea give this awful man a room in her house? Now he would go in and out as he pleased, and could help himself to her valuables if he wanted to.

Her silent indignation seemed to amuse him. He gave her his familiar mocking salute and put Kwan Yin down. Then he went to a door beyond Jan's bedroom that she had thought was a closet, and opened it. Through it she could see the narrow flight of stairs that led steeply upward. Before he disappeared up the stairs, Eddie Marshall glanced pointedly at the image lying on its side.

"Who do you suppose Rose was?" he mused, and went off up the stairs.

Jan blinked and reached toward the matting again. So Eddie Marshall knew about the lettered words. Had he taken off all the matting when he had the image away from the house? she wondered — and glued it back on? She stared at the place where the stuck part started, but the glue did not look at all fresh. The edge beyond the loose place appeared to be old, dry glue that had been there a long time. The matting might come off altogether with a good pull. So absorbed was she in her study that she did not hear the door open behind her. She heard nothing of her great-grandmother's soft advance across the carpets, until the old lady spoke.

"I thought I heard voices, Janice. Did Mr. Chilton come?"

Once more Jan jumped — feeling as guilty as Eddie had suggested. Quickly she edged about on the floor to hide the china figure from the old lady's view.

"No," she said. "It was Eddie Marshall going up to the tower. Is he going to stay here for good, Miss Althea?"

"I hope not, child." The old lady came nearer, moving slowly on her canes. Once more she had put on her turquoise-blue robe, and looked a little like a china figure herself. "He has no money and no place to go — since his father won't let him come home. I said he could stay here for a few days until he can get on his feet and find a room somewhere else. I meant to tell you, but I seem to forget so many things these days."

"Miss Althea," Jan said in a tense voice, and paused because the words faltered on her tongue. In a moment her great-grandmother would be close enough to see the image and it would be better to explain what she had done before Miss Althea spied it for herself.

She was too late. As she hesitated, Miss Althea's gaze swept past to the table beyond. Jan closed her eyes and braced herself, remembering how angry the old lady had sounded when she had caught her eavesdropping last night. Perhaps this would be the last straw. Perhaps she would be banished downstairs again, where she would have no room of her own. Or sent off to Boston to a Miss Minchin sort of school when fall came.

She could hear the swish of Miss Althea's silken gown as she came close, and smell the faint perfume that she used — that scent of sandalwood.

"I see you have once more succumbed to temptation, Janice?" Miss Althea said.

Jan opened her eyes, watching her great-grandmother fearfully.

"To succumb — " Miss Althea said, "to sink down, to yield, to give way. There are some wordbooks on that shelf over there. I suggest that you acquaint yourself with them. I have no intention of talking down to you as if you were a baby. There is an exact word for every occasion and you cannot hold your own in the world unless you learn to move with ease and understanding in the province of words. So let no word you don't understand escape you."

This was all very sensible, but at the moment Jan's main worry lay elsewhere. "I had to look at the idol," she said. "Dad told me there was a mystery and I — I wanted to find out about it."

"And have you?" the old lady demanded.

For the first time Jan brightened a little. "Maybe I have, Miss Althea. If you'll let me show you — "

"I'm too old for mysteries and secrets and surprises," her great-grandmother said. "I want you to show me

nothing. Take the dreadful old thing and put it back where it belongs."

Jan reached toward the loose corner of the matting. "But there's something so strange—"

"This instant!" said Miss Althea in a tone of such command that Jan jumped to her feet, picked up the idol, and carried it back to the chair that stood near the corner. When she had climbed upon it and put the image back, with its horrid expression turned toward the wall, she got down and faced her great-grandmother, more than a little frightened.

"I do hope," said the old lady, lowering herself into a chair, "that you are not going to prove a completely disrupting element in my life if I let you stay in my guest room. I did not like your listening at your door last night. I let the matter go this morning only because I don't feel strong enough to deal with such discourteous behavior. And now there is this! I can only hope that you won't dream about that ugly face and start screaming in the middle of the night. It has happened before. I've done it myself. However, you might as well sit down and stop fidgeting. We both need to compose ourselves for Mr. Chilton's visit. I will thank you not to mention this particular monster while he is here."

Jan had no wish to mention it to anyone. She felt as thoroughly chastised as though she had been a small child who had just received a spanking. Her great-grandmother was right, and Jan Pendleton was wrong, and yet—and yet—

Mr. Chilton's arrival brought a halt to thoughts of her own guilt. She was very subdued and said nothing at all while he was there. Mr. Chilton seemed pleased with the choice they had set out for him, and he took the trouble to thank Jan warmly when Miss Althea explained that she had made the selection. His one disappointment was that he could not borrow Kwan Yin.

"Of course I would never set her among the monsters," he said, "although she might have a benign influence upon them."

"Perhaps another time," Miss Althea said gently. "Now I must bargain with you. If you'd really like to display these things in your Oriental exhibit, I have one request to make."

"Of course." Mr. Chilton nodded. "Anything you like, Mrs. Pendleton."

Miss Althea's smile was the rather secretive one she wore when she meant to take someone by surprise, so Jan knew something unexpected was coming.

"Janice," the old lady said, "will you go to the foot of the stairs, please, and ask Eddie Marshall to come down for a moment."

Jan did as she was told, and Eddie appeared so quickly that she felt sure he had been near the door, doing his best to listen. He was a fine one to talk about other people eavesdropping!

"Mr. Chilton," Miss Althea went on, "I'm sure you remember Eddie Marshall. He has come home and is staying with us for a little while. We've managed to give him a few odd jobs around the house, but he is going to need more work than we can furnish. I wonder if you could find him something to do over at the Seaport."

It was to Mr. Chilton's credit that he did not look in the least disconcerted, nor did he have anything for Eddie but a friendly smile as he held out his hand.

"I'll see what I can do," he said when they had shaken hands. "Your grandfather is an old and good friend of mine and I know your future is of concern to him. I'll speak to a few people and see what can be worked out."

For once Eddie lost his mocking look. He seemed abashed by Mr. Chilton and thanked the older man rather awkwardly before hurrying out. It occurred to Jan that the last thing Eddie Marshall seemed to expect from anyone was kindness. Both he and his brother Patrick seemed to wear very large chips on their shoulders most of the time.

When Mr. Chilton had packed the porcelains and jade into a carton of excelsior he had brought, and taken them out to his car, Miss Althea settled in her chair and closed her eyes with an air of withdrawing from all further exertion. It was then that Jan remembered Neil and the request he had charged her with. So much had been happening that she had forgotten it completely. Probably this was the wrong time to ask, since Miss Althea was displeased with her, but she had better try before the old lady was sound asleep.

"Miss Althea—" She hesitated, not at all sure of her ground.

Her great-grandmother opened her eyes and Jan faltered on.

"Neil Kent—the boy next door—has a very interesting hobby. He was—showing it to me, and—"

Miss Althea allowed her eyes to close again, and Jan hurried, her words beginning to tumble.

"Neil records interviews with—with interesting people and he asked me to find out—that is—if you would let him talk to you."

This time Miss Althea did not trouble to open her eyes. "Certainly not," she said, and drifted gently off to sleep.

That was the end of that. Jan turned and tiptoed out of the room. There was nothing to do but tell Neil that his request had been definitely refused. She felt disappointed, both because attending the recording would be something interesting to do, and also because Neil would probably blame her for Miss Althea's refusal. Apparently she was going to have a hard time gaining anyone's approval, let alone friendship or love.

There—she had done it again! How long did homesickness last, anyway?

10 EDDIE LOSES HIS TEMPER

THE NEXT FEW days went by quietly enough. Neil, as Jan had expected, was not pleased about Miss Althea's refusal to let him interview her. He coaxed Jan to ask the old lady again, but this she would not do. Miss Althea was not the sort of person you could tease into doing anything and Jan had no wish to irritate her further. Indeed, she was trying to move with the greatest caution.

"I wish *I* could have talked to her," Neil said. "I'll bet I could get her to say yes. You probably did it all wrong."

Jan had no defense for that. Quite possibly this was true, but there was nothing further she could do for the moment.

During this brief period of quiet she visited the Seaport again and saw many more of the exhibits and museums. The place was endlessly fascinating and when added together made up a picture of a large slice of American history that was not so very long past.

Whether Mr. Chilton had found work for Eddie to do, Jan did not learn. It was part of staying out of trouble to ask no questions. Sometimes Eddie disappeared for long stretches of time, but she had to admit that he seemed to work very hard when he was around the house. He had even enlisted Jan's help in digging up dandelions and crabgrass on the weedy front lawn. With Gran's permission he brought in a load of earth and fertilizer and planted new grass seed. Then he strung strands of string between little wooden posts to discourage children and dogs from running across the newly seeded stretch of lawn.

When he was working Eddie seemed a different person. He did not talk at all, but concentrated so thoroughly on what he was doing and worked with such care that it seemed as though he must be trying to prove something. Whether to himself or to Miss Althea or to the world in general, Jan did not know. At least he was less unpleasant while busy and everyone, including Jan herself, began to relax about him to some degree. Miss Althea said that keeping him busy was clearly the solution. Gran and Mrs. Marshall seemed pleasantly surprised, and sometimes Patrick dropped over to watch his brother and to help him when he had spare time of his own.

Only Neil remained skeptical. Several times Jan saw him watching from the Kent front yard — which could have done with some weeding itself. More than once he said, "You wait. There'll be trouble yet — you'll see."

When trouble finally came, however, it was Neil himself who caused the whole calamity. To be fair, as Jan tried to be later, what happened was not intentional. Neil was thinking of something else and he simply forgot about Eddie's neat and freshly seeded lawn.

Mr. Kent had brought home a puppy for his son the day before. It was a half-grown cocker spaniel, lively and mischievous and ready for trouble. Neil could hardly have been happier, and Jan was summoned over several times to pet and admire the little dog. Neil had consulted her about naming it, and Jan was pleased because this meant he had forgiven her failure with Miss Althea. Not that Neil took any of the suggestions she offered, though he allowed her to agree over his final choice. Sunburst was to be the little fellow's name. As Neil said, he wanted something different that would get away from the usual doggy names. This name struck him when he watched the noonday sunlight brighten the darker patches on the puppy's coat so that they glowed a bright red-gold — almost like Patrick's hair. Of course in no time at all Neil had shortened this to Sunny — which, Jan felt, wasn't too different from the usual sort of name for a dog.

On this particular morning Miss Althea had invited Jan to visit with her awhile, and they were sitting on the upstairs front porch. The old lady was telling her the fascinating story of a time when Jan's father had come to visit her in this house as a little boy.

Eddie Marshall was out in front of the house watering the newly seeded lawn, careful to stand well outside its boundaries in order not to step on the fresh loam. There was the usual putt-putt of boats on the river, and the lazy chirp of an occasional bird. Next door Sunny was barking furiously as he engaged in some game with his new master. Otherwise the morning was quiet and peaceful.

But not for very long. Sunny was already learning how to trick his owner, and as Jan sat looking idly down through the railings of the porch, the dog suddenly wriggled out of Neil's grasp and went streaking for the road where cars went by. Eddie's string and small stakes did not deter him at all. He simply floundered over a section of string with his clumsy puppy feet and made tracks right across the fresh earth of the lawn. Then he squeezed between strands of the second barrier and was happily off toward the middle of the road.

Neil saw only the dog and its danger. He snatched up his bicycle, got onto it, and rode straight after his pet — a course that took him directly over the new lawn, breaking down neat strands of string as he went and leaving deep furrows in the earth. Eddie, hose in hand, let out a yell of fury and turned the stream of water right into Neil's face. Everything happened so quickly that Jan, who had jumped up to stand at the rail and was watching in horror, hadn't time to say a word.

Neil, blinded by the water, fell off his bike and made a muddy mess of both himself and the lawn. Eddie cast the hose aside and leaped into the ring after him, pulled him to his feet and began to shake him with such concentrated anger that Neil cowered in fear and tried to protect himself.

Jan heard herself crying out, "Stop it, Eddie! Stop it!"

It was Miss Althea who made him stop. She stood at the rail beside Jan and spoke in a voice that carried clearly, though it was low and not at all frantic.

"Edward Marshall!" Miss Althea said. And then again, "Edward Marshall!"

Perhaps nothing else, short of force, could have stopped Eddie in the punishment he was inflicting upon Neil. But Miss Althea's commanding tone was a voice out of the past. The voice of authority. It penetrated his blind anger and he let Neil go and stepped back. Released, Neil fled for the safety of his own house, not daring to look behind. Sunny, having discovered that he was not to be chased, floundered back across the now torn up and muddy lawn and rejoined his master. Jan heard the distant slam of a door as Neil and the dog disappeared inside.

Eddie stood looking at the wreckage of all his painstaking work. He did not look up at Miss Althea at all.

The old lady spoke to him again, quietly, firmly. "No matter what happens, you can't afford to behave like that, Eddie. Your temper will be the ruin of you. Any trouble you get into now may cause your parole to be revoked, as you very well know."

Eddie shook his head back and forth several times, as if trying to clear away the fog of rage. He still did not look at the two who watched him from the upper porch, but went up the walk and sat down on the steps, just out of sight.

Jan heard his mother speaking to him, chiding him from below. She turned to Miss Althea. "Neil's father is going to be awfully angry. He already knows Eddie was in jail, and Neil says he doesn't like having him around the neighborhood."

"Let's go inside," Miss Althea said.

The strength lent by necessity had faded and she looked suddenly old and fragile as she leaned on her canes. Indoors Jan helped her settle into her chair and for once the old lady did not push away her offer of help.

"Everything is too much for me," the old lady said. "I simply cannot allow him to stay here. Wherever he is he breeds trouble. I can't face this sort of thing anymore. I'm too old. I only want to be left alone."

There was a sound of steps on the stairs and Jan looked anxiously toward the door. Mrs. Marshall tapped and came in hurriedly. She rushed at once to Miss Althea.

"I've been afraid something would happen ever since

Eddie came home," she wailed. "But he seemed to be doing so well, and I had hoped everything would change."

Miss Althea shook her head wearily without speaking.

"It wasn't Eddie's fault in the beginning," Jan put in, wanting to be fair. "Neil shouldn't have ridden across the lawn. But I saw the whole thing and I don't think he knew what he was doing."

"I'm afraid who is to blame doesn't make any difference now." Mrs. Marshall spoke sadly. "It's the trouble the Kents may make for Eddie that is serious. I wish Patrick had been here. He might have prevented this. He might have—"

Miss Althea recovered herself to a degree and interrupted. "There is no use in idle wishing, Mary dear. I wonder if we could persuade Mrs. Kent to come over and see me. Perhaps I could have a little talk with her so that I could explain and apologize."

That wouldn't do much good, Jan thought, if Neil chose to play up his injury to his parents, and held back the fact of his own misbehavior, as he was quite likely to do. He had a way of exaggerating things, and this story was bad enough to start with.

A sudden inspiration struck her. "I know what you could do!" she told Miss Althea.

The old lady regarded her with interest. "What do you have in mind, Janice?"

"There's that taped interview Neil is so anxious to make," Jan said. "If you'd give him permission to bring over his recorder and ask you questions, maybe he won't make such a fuss about what happened. His mother isn't home. I saw her go out in the car. I could run over and talk to him before he says anything to his parents."

Miss Althea considered this soberly. "What you are suggesting is that we attempt to bribe the boy for his silence?"

Jan gulped. She had not thought of it like that. "I don't mean that, exactly. It's just that he won't do so much harm if he's not mad. After all, it was his fault to start with."

Her great-grandmother reached out and patted her gently on the arm. "You're rather like your father at times. He had an enterprising imagination as a boy. I do believe you've given us a good idea. In so important a cause a little smoothing of the ego may be indicated. I'll give the Kent boy an interview, if you wish. In fact, I'll do anything I can—except keep Eddie on in this house." She turned to Mrs. Marshall. "You do understand, Mary?"

Mrs. Marshall looked pink around the eyes again. "I understand very well. I don't blame you in the least."

"Thank you," Miss Althea said. "I expect Patrick will be the one who will think I've let Eddie down and will scold me. But never mind that. Run along, Janice, and see if you can mend the rift in our defenses."

Jan ran downstairs and out the side door. She felt eager and excited about having a chance to help, and she tingled with pleasure over her great-grandmother's praise. Only a tiny misgiving tapped at the back of her mind, and she would not listen or let it in.

As she crossed the driveway, she saw that Patrick Marshall was on the dock tying up his boat. It was a shame he had arrived too late.

If he had been earlier, he might have seen how badly his older brother could behave. Jan, however, had no desire to tell him what had happened, and she hurried on her way, not looking back until she reached Neil's front porch. A glance over her shoulder told her that Patrick had gone straight to the Pendleton house.

At Neil's door she rang the bell breathlessly several times. Inside, the little dog began to bark, having already begun his duties as watchdog, as well as mischief-maker. After a considerable wait Neil came to the door. His hair was wet and slicked down and his face looked pink from both scrubbing and anger. He had changed to clean dungarees and shirt and looked increasingly furious. At his heels the puppy gamboled, an innocent cause of all the trouble.

"What do you want?" Neil asked rudely.

Jan stood her ground. "You don't need to shout at me. I haven't hurt you. I'm only here to do you a favor."

"Thanks for nothing," Neil said. "You can have your favors! I don't want anything from people who hire convicts and let them push other people around. Boy! wait till I tell my dad! He'll get that friend of yours run out of town fast."

This was exactly what Jan had feared would be Neil's attitude. "He isn't a friend of mine," she went on doggedly, "and I don't think my great-grandmother will allow him to stay after what has happened. We both saw the whole thing from the upstairs porch and she's terribly upset."

"She ought to be!" Neil snapped. "So will my dad be. *And* my mother."

Sunny began to leap eagerly around Jan's ankles and she bent to pick him up and snuggle him against her cheek. She had no answer for Neil's words and merely waited for him to run down.

"What did you come over for?" he asked at last.

Jan tried another direction. "Of course your father will be angry with Eddie for losing his temper. But Eddie had a reason, so I guess your dad will be annoyed with you too. You had no business riding over a lawn that had a guard around it and had just been seeded. You could easily have gone around."

Neil thought about that for a moment. Then he reached out and took Sunny from her, as if he did not want to see the little dog showing affection for the enemy. A thoughtful, rather wary look had come into his eyes.

Jan went on quietly, pushing her advantage. "My great-grandmother sent me over to tell you how sorry we all are about what Eddie did. If you still want that interview, she will give it to you in order to make up for what happened."

Neil continued to look thoughtful, while Sunny licked eagerly at his cheek. After a moment he seemed to make up his mind.

"Maybe I won't tell Dad after all," he said. "Maybe I'd rather take care of this myself."

Somehow that had an ominous ring, and for the first time the tapping of doubt in Jan's mind began to make itself heard. What if she managed to arrange this interview and then Neil did something awful that would make everything worse? In that case she herself might be to blame, might find herself in real trouble. Yet there was nothing else to do but take this chance, and she once more pushed doubt away. After all, remembering how frightened Neil had been of Eddie, she did not think he was likely to stand up to him later. And there was nothing serious he could do during the recording, with Miss Althea right there. She let his veiled threat go unchallenged.

"When do you want to bring over your tape recorder?" she asked.

This time Neil gave in completely. His hobby took first place with him, as Jan had hoped it would.

"How about tomorrow morning around ten?" he asked."

"I'll ask my great-grandmother and let you know." Jan did not linger lest he change his mind, but started down the steps.

He called after her. "If I talk to Mrs. Pendleton, I'm going to find out about that idol! I'm not going to stay off any subject I want to ask about."

Jan merely nodded and hurried away. Was it in this direction that trouble might develop? Surely such questions would be up to Miss Althea, and Jan suspected that the old lady would handle the interview exactly as she pleased.

She felt a little better as she returned to the Pendleton house. Eddie had disappeared, she noted, as she climbed the outside stairs and entered her great-grandmother's living room. Mrs. Marshall still hovered watchfully over the old lady, and now Patrick was there too. Apparently he had been told the whole story because an angry flush shaded right up through his freckles, to be lost in his red hair. Maybe it was a good thing he hadn't been here to help Eddie out after all, Jan thought. There might have been a real fight.

"If it's all right with you, Neil wants to bring over his tape recorder at ten o'clock tomorrow morning," she announced at once, feeling a little triumphant over what she had achieved.

Miss Althea nodded. "That will be fine. I like people who use their heads," she told Jan. "I'm thankful that you thought of this. While Eddie must certainly learn to hold his temper, it is terribly important for him not to get into trouble at this time."

Jan went out on the side stairs and called to Neil, who was waiting on his own steps for an answer. When she had told him that ten o'clock was all right, she came inside to find Patrick staring at her suspiciously.

"What's all this about a tape recorder?" he asked.

Once more she explained Neil's hobby and how he wanted to tape an interview with Great-grandmother Althea.

Patrick's eyes widened. "Are you nuts? I wouldn't trust that guy any farther than I could throw an outboard motor! All he wants is to show off and prove how important he is."

Jan winced and the tap of worry in her mind turned into a thump. Surely Neil would never try anything funny around her great-grandmother, but she could not be sure.

Miss Althea frowned her disapproval of Patrick. "I don't think so unforgiving and prejudiced an attitude is going to help."

Patrick had the grace to look slightly ashamed. "Anyway," he said, "I'd like to be here for the interview. Then I can keep an eye on Neil Kent."

"You may come," said Miss Althea, "only if you will be civil to him and not make everything worse. Is that agreed?"

Patrick nodded, but Jan did not like the resentment for Neil that smoldered in his eyes. She was beginning to grow more and more worried about the coming interview.

"I'll be glad to have you here, Patrick," Miss Althea went on. "Perhaps you can help me if this young man's questions become importunate."

The word caught Jan's attention and distracted her from her concern. She repeated it to herself. *Importunate.* She liked the feeling of a new word on her tongue, and this was an interesting one. How would Neil behave if he became "importunate"?

"Go look it up," Miss Althea said, observing her knowingly.

Jan grinned and went off to the dictionary. "Trouble-somely urgent," she found, and "overpressing in request." Yes, Neil was likely to be all those things. On the other hand such an approach might make for an interesting interview, since there were questions to which she would like to hear Miss Althea give the answers. Further questions about the Chinese idol, for instance.

When Patrick and Mrs. Marshall had gone downstairs, Jan was left to herself. Once she went outside and looked over the porch rail to see that Eddie was back in sight and working doggedly at repairing the damage to his lawn. Patrick stood on the walk talking to him. When Eddie glanced up and saw Jan, he stared at her coldly until she withdrew from the rail, not liking the look in his eyes.

She supposed that Patrick must have told his brother about the planned interview and he probably did not approve of it either. Which wasn't fair, since the whole purpose of the plan was to help Eddie Marshall. And it should help — provided nothing went wrong. The thought of things that might go wrong, considering both Neil's and Patrick's personalities, was upsetting.

An idea was beginning to build in Jan's mind, and for the rest of the day and well into the evening, she thought about it. How dramatic and exciting it would be — and how interesting for Neil's interview — if the answer to the mystery of the idol could come out during the taping. If she could produce something really surprising, Neil would be so pleased that he would forget all about trying to get even with Eddie and Patrick. *Tap!* went the warning sound at the back of her mind, but she did not listen at all, caught up wholeheartedly in working out this new notion.

By nighttime she was well into a pleasant fantasy. She would wait until Miss Althea's answers to Neil's questions faltered, since not even Miss Althea knew the full solution to the mystery. Into this pause Jan would speak quietly, to announce the words of the hidden message pressed into the clay base of the idol. However, she could do this only if, in the meantime, she found out what the full message said.

At bedtime her delight in this plan, coupled with her curiosity, had grown into something she must take action about soon. It would be wonderful to astonish everyone — and would present Miss Althea with knowledge that would be valuable to her in some way, even after all these years.

For a while she sat up in bed reading further into the story of Sara Crewe. Sara's father was dead by this time in the narrative, and her life was terribly sad. But the mysterious Indian gentleman, Ram Dass, had appeared on the scene, and the story was so absorbing that Jan was able to get her mind off her own problems for a little while.

When she put the book aside and lay down, ready at last for sleep, she did what she had found herself able to do on certain occasions in the past. She set a make-believe alarm in her own mind for midnight. By that time Miss Althea would probably be asleep. There would be no danger of discovery that late at night. She would simply get the idol and bring it to her room. When she knew whatever there was to be known about the rest of the message, she would put it back. A very simple plan. She would then be ready to make a contribution of her own to Neil's recording at ten o'clock tomorrow morning.

She willed herself to go to sleep at once, so the time would come quickly for the exciting discovery, and fortunately, she was sleepy enough so that this was exactly what she did.

In the depths of the house the grandfather clock ticked away the minutes one by one, and Jan, at last, lay sound asleep.

11 THE REST
OF THE MESSAGE

AS HAD HAPPENED most times before when she had told herself when to wake up, Jan wakened very near the appointed hour. What was more, she knew at once why she was awake. Very quietly she slipped out of bed, turning on no lights. In her bare feet she went to the door and put her hand on its knob. She opened the door without making a sound. She was cautious, however, and opened it scarcely a hair's breadth in order to make sure her great-grandmother was not up and around. This was a very good thing.

The voices had been so subdued that she had not heard the whisper of them with her door closed. Lamps were on in the living room, and out of sight at the rear Miss Althea was talking to someone. Just as Jan was about to close the door, her great-grandmother raised her voice to answer some argument, and this time Jan heard the words.

"This is what you must do," the old lady said. "There isn't any other way. Do you understand?"

The reply was mumbled, indistinct. As softly as she had opened her door, Jan closed it and skipped back to bed. She had eavesdropped once — and in spite of a burning curiosity, she must not do so again. It was undoubtedly Eddie Marshall out there talking to Miss Althea. She would have to postpone her expedition of discovery until still later that night. How long the two would stay up talking, there was no way to tell. She might as well go back to sleep.

Though she set herself no definite time to waken, nevertheless, two hours later she came suddenly awake again and remembered that her mission was yet to be completed. Downstairs the grandfather clock bonged the hour of two. This time it was harder to come awake, but her plan had to be carried out and she made herself get out of bed. She could only hope that this was not one of those nights when Miss Althea suffered from insomnia way into the morning.

The door opened a crack at her cautious touch, and beyond, all was silent. Only a shaded Chinese lantern that Miss Althea liked to leave burning all night cast a dim yellow glow, and Jan was grateful for what light it shed as she made her way down the long expanse of the room. The Chinese carpets felt thick and soft beneath her feet, as if she were walking on warm grass.

Her great-grandmother's bedroom door stood ajar and Jan paused fearfully. She would have to step into plain view of that open door in order to take the idol down. As she hesitated she heard the light, soft sound of steady, rhythmic breathing coming from the bedroom's darkness. Miss Althea was sound asleep.

Luckily the chair on which Jan had climbed to get the idol down the first time had not been put back in the kitchen. She stepped up on it in her bare feet and reached toward the shadowy shelf. For an instant as she touched the cold china of the figure a little shiver went through her and she was glad its back was turned. She could never have endured the awful look of that face peering at her in this yellowish light. If only she could manage what had to be done without looking at its face at all.

The thing seemed heavier than before in her hands and she thought how awful it would be if it slipped through her fingers and went crashing to the floor. She managed to hold onto the fat body tightly as she got down from the chair with the utmost care. The distance back to her room seemed endless, but she made it safely, with no change to be heard in the sound of that light breathing.

Not until her door was closed and the image dumped on the bed did she dare to turn on a light and give her full attention to the figure of the idol.

While it lay with its ugly face pressed into the bed-clothes, Jan began to poke and pry at the straw matting that covered the base. At first it was hard to get hold of a large enough piece to give it a real pull, but she finally loosened enough to get a good grip on one corner. After that it was easy. With two or three pulls, the whole thing came off in her hand with a loud ripping noise that made her hold her breath lest she had wakened the whole house. But no one stirred.

She had been right. There was more to the message — if that was what it was. Across the under part of the figure several words had been cut into the clay.

Jan brought the idol closer to the bed-table lamp, pushed its face away from her into a pillow and bent to examine the words. They were upside down and she could not read them. There was no help for it — she would have to turn the monster over. She did so gingerly and then of course she had to look right into the dreadful face.

It was an eerie experience with the reading lamp glowing upon the popping eyes and fanged snarl of the dreadful thing. Jan had a sudden sharp awareness that she was the only soul awake in the house—that she was truly alone with something monstrously evil. What if that grinning, lipless mouth should gnash at her? What if the eyes should roll?

Then common sense flooded back in a reassuring wave. Oh, stop it! she told herself, knowing perfectly well that there was something faintly enjoyable about scaring herself like this. She reached out to put a hand over the glaring face and gave it a rude shove.

"You're only an ugly old piece of china," she said— and was not bitten for her words.

She bent again to examine the base of the figure. The letters were rather crudely made, as if someone had used a pointed instrument hastily to write in wet clay, but they were perfectly clear. She read the message in a soft whisper to herself:

"*For Rose of Sharon—find a happy heart.*"

There it was—and that was all. Who Rose of Sharon was she did not know—except that it was a phrase out of the Bible. The words "happy heart" must refer to the article Grandpa Marshall had told her about—the one Gillespie Osborn had written about happiness. This might have been a last message to someone when he realized that he could not get away from Shanghai alive. In that case it should please Miss Althea to have the words presented to her, even though, as far as Jan was concerned, the solution to the mystery seemed pretty disappointing. At least it would be fun to reveal what she had discovered during the recorded interview, and perhaps Miss Althea could make something of it.

Now she must return the idol to its high perch. She was less concerned about its ugly face than when she had brought it to her room. Having looked at it boldly, she was no longer afraid of it.

Putting it back offered no problem, except for one thing. There was no way of fastening the matting securely in place and she could only hope that no one would investigate before it was time to get the figure down and show it to her great-grandmother during the recording. Miss Althea could not refuse to look at it then.

At least nothing squeaked unduly, nor did she bump into anything on the way or drop the china figure. Miss Althea's even breathing told Jan that she was still asleep. There was no sound from the tower overhead, and the door to Eddie's room remained closed. When the idol had been set firmly on its mat, she went back to bed and fell sound asleep almost at once.

She hardly stirred until well after eight o'clock the next morning, and she found herself sleepy for a long while after she had risen.

The morning proved to be a busy one because Miss Althea was full of directions as to how everything must be arranged for the interview. If there had been anything unpleasant about her talk with Eddie, she did not betray the fact, and she seemed to have thrown off her disturbed feelings of yesterday. Indeed, the prospect of something unusual happening seemed to stimulate, rather than to tire her.

Today the old lady wore another of her long gowns of Hong Kong silk, this one a jade green with a pattern of bamboo leaves scattered across it. Her white hair was coiled at the back of her head, as always, and tortoise-shell combs with gold backs held the coils in place. She looked younger today, it seemed to Jan, and her eyes had a green sparkle to them as if they had picked up the hue of the gown. Jan could only hope that nothing would happen to spoil this air of interest and eagerness that became her so well.

Gran came up to see how everything was going before she went to work, and it was clear that she did not like the idea of this interview. Before she left, she took Jan aside and spoke to her soberly.

"Do keep an eye on your great-grandmother," she said. "If she seems to be tiring, or if anything upsetting happens, try to stop this and send the boys home."

Jan had no confidence about being able to do any such thing, but she promised doubtfully to try.

Patrick arrived early and was helpful about moving furniture about to suit Miss Althea. As Jan assisted him, she soon realized that there was a friendship of long standing between the old lady and the boy. They seemed comfortable with each other — as though, Jan thought, remembering Miss Althea's first words to her, each knew *who* the other was. She wished she could be as much at ease with her great-grandmother, but she still felt awed by the old lady, and often uncertain of how Miss Althea would react. Patrick was far less prickly with her, as if he knew that the chip-on-the-shoulder attitude he presented to the rest of the world was not needed with Miss Althea. Indeed, he even treated Jan less gruffly in the old lady's presence than he had before, and she began to feel more and more encouraged about the coming interview.

Only once was there a moment of antagonism on Patrick's part, and that was when Miss Althea explained that she had told Eddie last night that he must leave the house, and that she hoped, for the good of his family and friends, that Eddie would leave town altogether and make a new life for himself in some place where no one knew him.

"Why should he?" Patrick asked boldly. "This is where he ought to find friends who will help him and want to see him get back on his feet."

Miss Althea answered him gently, without taking offense. "I wish human nature were like that, but I'm afraid it's not. Society often refuses to forgive our mistakes or to let them die. Then recovery becomes too difficult where everyone knows us. It's easier to become someone new when you're far away from home. In a sense you can shed your old skin that way."

Patrick scowled as he thought about this. "Eddie doesn't need to be someone new. He wasn't guilty of what they sent him to prison for. He told me so himself."

Miss Althea regarded him sadly. "There was a trial, and as you know, my daughter-in-law and I saw to it that Eddie had a good lawyer, since your father wasn't working at the time. The men Eddie was with testified against him, and there were witnesses besides. I don't think we should try to fool ourselves about this."

For a moment Patrick looked so angry that Jan thought he would turn around and stamp out of Miss Althea's apartment. But at that moment Neil arrived, carrying his portable recorder and the flight bag in which he kept his equipment. At sight of him, Patrick abruptly changed his mind. He and Neil greeted each other with surly reluctance and it was clear that only Miss Althea's presence caused them to speak to each other at all.

Neil set the recorder on the low, round table Miss Althea had cleared for it. From his flight bag he took tapes and microphone and other odds and ends of professional equipment and made the necessary connections. Then he rearranged the chairs around the table so that he could sit close to Miss Althea and pass the microphone back and forth between them. Patrick and Jan sat opposite, since they would not be taking part in the interview. At least, that was what Neil believed, but Jan felt a pleasant tingling run through her at the thought of the unexpected part she meant to play.

More than once that morning she had glanced at the idol, safe on its shelf, with its green-robed back to the room. No one had found out about the loosened mat. The chair still stood handy for getting him down when the time came. Once Patrick tried to carry the chair to the kitchen, but Jan prevented that by sitting down in it quickly and bending over to look at books in a nearby bookcase.

When Neil had made a voice test and found that Miss Althea's voice recorded pleasantly and distinctly, the in-

terview began. Jan listened with interest and some surprise. Neil knew how to do an expert job. He had thought
out his main questions ahead of time, but he was also
quick to encourage Miss Althea to talk when she came to
some interesting phase of her experiences. At the same
time, he kept her on the track, bringing her gently back to
the point if she wandered. Altogether, he showed himself
to be far more courteous and thoughtful than Jan would
have believed possible.

The old lady spoke easily and without self-conscious-
ness, though she had probably never used a microphone
before. This particular story came easily to her lips, and
Neil's flattering attention drew her on. Before Jan quite
realized how he had managed it, Neil had brought the

talk around to the time when Gillespie Osborn had sent his daughter to Chinese friends for safety, hoping to follow her later on. Miss Althea told about how the best of the jade collection — at least all the smaller things — had been packed in the handbag she carried, and how she had eventually been able to bring them home to the States with her.

"Did he give you that old idol to carry with you at the same time?" Neil inquired when Mrs. Pendleton paused, her eyes shadowed and dreamy as they looked into the past. Jan held her breath, but the old lady was not angry.

As though the question were perfectly natural, and without asking Neil how he knew about the idol, she went right on talking. She told of how Gillespie Osborn, for some reason of his own — probably out of friendship for the man who had made the figure so long ago — had chosen to send the ugly thing to her to bring home when she left.

"It was easy enough to get it to me," she said. "Our Chinese servant was stopped once or twice on the way to the house where I was hiding, but anyone could tell that the monstrous thing had no value, so they let him pass. I suppose it wasn't even worth smashing, and they probably respected its purpose as a temple guardian."

Neil threw a quick, sly look at Jan, as if to say that he was quite pleased with himself over getting her to tell the story. He put his next question casually.

"Didn't you have any notion yourself of why he sent the idol for you to bring home?"

This time Miss Althea answered testily as though he had irked her. "I do wish you would stop calling it an idol. It isn't anything of the sort. An idol is something put up in a temple for people to worship. My friend on the shelf up there has a totally different use. Patrick, will you get him down for me, please? I might as well introduce him on Neil's interview."

The moment had come all too suddenly, but before Patrick could move, Jan jumped to her feet and ran to the corner herself. She did not want anyone to know about the straw mat being loose. She lifted the figure down carefully, experienced at this by now, and set him with equal care beside the tape recorder, safely resting on his mat. Neil had stopped the tape, waiting until Jan brought the figure to the table and turned its snarling face to confront him. She had the satisfaction of seeing Neil recoil for just an instant. Patrick showed no expression at all, so undoubtedly he had seen its face before.

"He's not a very handsome-looking chap, is he?" Miss Althea went on when Neil started the machine again. "But although you can call him a monster if you like, he isn't an idol and never was. Had he been placed near a Chinese temple, his function would have been to frighten off whatever evil spirits dared to come around. He would have been used for the same thing in a home. Apparently evil spirits are rather stupid and easily fooled. They can only move in a straight line, for instance, so if you place a barrier behind the opening in a gate, they lack the sense to go around it, as human beings do. Or so the Chinese used to claim. How such spirits look I don't know, but they are apparently frightened of ugly faces like this one. The friend who made the image for my father—I was only a child at the time—assured him that it would keep him safe forever from any wicked spirit who might come around."

"It didn't help him to escape safely, did it?" Neil said when Miss Althea paused.

"You forget—he sent it to me," she countered sadly. "In any case, it's not spirits who cause evil. It is only foolish men who kill each other."

Jan had not seated herself at the table when she put the figure down. She felt nervous now, and keyed up and eager. At any moment she would speak about her discovery into that very microphone, and now she was too edgy to sit still. She took a quick turn toward the front of the room and then started back to the table. In turning, she became aware of something she had not noticed before.

The door to the tower room stairs was open. The open door barred the stairs from the sight of those around the table at the back of the room, but Jan had a clear view of the steps. Eddie Marshall had not left the house after all. He was sitting right there on the bottom step, where he could hear everything that was said during the interview. What was more, he looked straight at Jan, as he caught her gaze upon him, and winked at her boldly, a finger to his lips.

Her reaction was one of shock and dismay. Everything had been going well—with Neil and Patrick both behaving themselves. But if Neil guessed that Eddie was here, listening in, the fat might really be in the fire.

Eddie seemed to sense her alarm and he shook his head, scowling as fiercely as Patrick. The scowl was clearly a threat. He did not look at all good-natured, in spite of the wink, and she felt suddenly frightened. She glanced uneasily toward the table and saw that Miss Althea was watching her. By making a real effort, Jan pretended to study a picture on the wall near the tower door, walking slowly back to the table as she did so.

Miss Althea returned her attention to Neil's questioning. "Yes, of course I wondered why my father had sent me the ugly thing. I know he was fond of the man who made it, and who had died long since. Perhaps he merely wanted to have this memento of his old friend when he himself left China, as he hoped to do. Or perhaps he was giving me something to protect me from evil spirits — as a sort of joke. Sometimes I was never quite sure how much Chinese lore my father had come to believe, being as deeply immersed in it as he was. There were other times when I wondered if it was supposed to convey some message to me — something my father wanted me to know, or to think about."

"That must have been it!" Jan cried, surprising herself as much as she did those around the table. She gulped as she found everyone staring at her, but she managed to go on. "There are words marked in the clay on the base of the figure. They were hidden by that old matting that's been stuck to it all the time. Look what I've found!"

She had forgotten about speaking into the microphone, but that no longer seemed to matter. She ran around the table and turned the figure on its back so the marking could be read. Neil leaned toward it in excitement, and this time it was he who read the words aloud:

"For Rose of Sharon — find a happy heart."

12 EDDIE
LISTENS IN

THERE WAS a brief silence in the room, while Jan watched her great-grandmother anxiously. What would the message mean to her? How would it change her thinking about the past?

"So that's the mystery," Neil said. "What does it mean?"

To Jan's surprise Miss Althea smiled ruefully. "History certainly keeps repeating itself. This has been going on for a very long while."

"What has been going on?" Jan looked in bewilderment from one face to another, and discovered that Patrick was laughing at her scornfully.

"That isn't any mystery," he said. "Everybody knows about the lettering on the bottom of the image."

Miss Althea spoke again, somewhat plaintively. "I suppose it's my own fault. I suppose the very way I've set the old thing up on a dark shelf and turned its face to the wall has made a mystery of it. As each younger generation comes along, sooner or later someone climbs up and tears off the matting to see what is underneath. And then—for me—the whole annoyance starts over again."

Crestfallen and disappointed, Jan could only sit in silence, leaving others to ask the questions.

"But what do the words mean?" Neil inquired.

"That has been a matter of speculation over the years," the old lady said. "Though I'm afraid I know well enough what it means and sometimes I've been furious with the old thing because of what it keeps telling me."

"Who is Rose of Sharon?" Jan found her tongue to ask.

Miss Althea gestured to the nearby bookcase. "You'll find a book of names on the top shelf. See if you can find the answer for yourself — since you're so interested in mystery-solving."

There was silence while Jan got the book, and once more Neil stopped the turning tape and set down the microphone he had been shoving at each of them in turn. When Jan found the book and brought it back to the table, she had no idea what to do with it. She looked up "Rose" and found merely that it was a flower name. And of course "Sharon" was a place name from the Bible. Having run out of ideas, she looked blankly at Miss Althea and found her nodding amused encouragement. Suddenly Jan knew what she meant. She turned the pages to "Althea," and there she found the answer.

"'Wholesome or healing (Greek),'" she read aloud. "'A flower name. The althea, or rose of Sharon, is a plant supposed to have medicinal power.'"

Again Miss Althea nodded. "When my father felt especially loving, or when he wanted to give me some advice he considered important, he used to call me 'Rose of Sharon.' That is why I'm sure it was he who wrote those words in the wet clay he must have smeared across the bottom of the image before he sent it to me. It was a message that would mean nothing to anyone else. Yet I'm afraid I know what it meant for me."

With a start Neil come to himself and turned on the tape. He had been so absorbed in what was happening that he had momentarily forgotten the interview.

"*Happy Heart*," Patrick said, "—that was the name of a sailboat, wasn't it?"

"It was indeed," the old lady agreed. "When I escaped from China after that last visit to my father, Randy and I examined the Chinese image together and of course we tore off the matting and discovered the lettering. I think Father put it there because I had trouble with my temper as a girl. And perhaps because there were always so many things I thought my happiness depended on—things I wanted. So he wished to leave me this last bit of advice. He knew I would remember some of the things he had preached."

"What things?" Neil asked bluntly.

"Don't parents always preach?" Miss Althea asked. "And doesn't each new generation refuse to listen until it grows up to wisdom itself? My father was a bit of a philosopher, and happiness—what it really means—happened to be one of his favorite subjects. I can remember his lecturing me about how it could never be a goal on ahead. It had to come right now, he said, and of course right now always depended on what I had done yesterday and the day before. It was all a bit complicated for me to understand when I was young."

Neil was not interested in a lecture on happiness. "Did you name the sailboat?" he asked, remembering that he was supposed to be putting questions to Althea Pendleton.

"Randy named her," Miss Althea said. "That was before we were married and he chose that name because he said I did have a happy heart. Of course he didn't know me as well at that time as he got to later on. Sometimes I've had anything but a happy heart and there have been times when I've wanted to throw something at that old china fellow because he kept reminding me of my father's words. But I couldn't throw him out or give him away, since he was the last thing my father ever sent me. So I turned his ugly face to the wall and put him in a dark corner where he wouldn't reproach me and tell me it was my own fault when things went wrong and I behaved badly. Even then, I couldn't forget him. I suppose, in a way, he has had a tremendous influence on my life — all because I loved my father very much and I did want to do what he expected of me. Especially when he was gone so suddenly and I would never see him again."

She brushed a hand across her face, as though she brushed away old and painful memories. Then she nodded at the figure.

"Let him stay down in the room, Janice. Put him wherever you like. And don't glue the matting back on. Perhaps this is the time when I need that message most of all."

Uncertainly Jan picked up the figure. Somehow she felt terribly disappointed. The answer to what had seemed an exciting mystery was nothing but a letdown. It didn't mean anything except a father telling his daughter how to be happy. What was worse, everyone had known about the message all along.

As she carried the figure toward a drop-front desk and set it on the top, she remembered the man on the stairs. Eddie Marshall was still there. He grinned when he saw the image in her hands and gave her a rather curious shake of his head. It was as if he was saying, "I don't believe a word of it. There *is* a mystery." But Jan did not like to have him there, listening, when his presence was not suspected. In this situation there were possibilities of trouble.

"On second thought," Miss Althea said, "I don't think I can bear to have that snarling look following me everywhere I go."

She pulled herself up from her chair and went to an Oriental chest of drawers with brass handles. From the top drawer she took a large square of black satin, embroidered with a wriggling gold dragon, and brought it to Jan.

"Here you are! Drape this over him. Then the two monsters can keep each other company." She was standing where she could see Eddie on the stairs, if she looked.

Jan took the square of embroidered satin and draped it over the image's head. It was large enough to cover the squat figure completely, so that the gold dragon was on display, instead of that snarling face.

Miss Althea turned about slowly and faced the tower door without surprise — as if she had known all along that he was there.

"I hope this has been an edifying hour for you," she said to the man on the stairs.

Eddie stayed where he was, not even troubling to look embarrassed. Miss Althea moved toward him across the room, holding herself straight in spite of her canes, and stood at the doorway to the tower. Patrick had jumped up from his place at the table and come quickly to where he too could see his brother. Jan glanced toward Neil and saw that he was the only one who had no interest in Eddie's appearance on the scene. As he put away his equipment he looked sulky and annoyed over the inter-

ruption that had ended his interview. Neil's moment of importance was over, and Jan forgot him as she watched what followed.

"I had hoped you would be well on your way out of town by now," Miss Althea said to Eddie. "I believe that is what we agreed upon last night."

Eddie seemed less afraid of Miss Althea today. He stood up, lounging indolently against the wall of the stairwell. "Old Chilton has got me that job at the Seaport, and I might as well work at it for a while before I leave."

"Very well," Miss Althea said, "but you cannot stay in this house another night. Your presence has been too disturbing for all of us."

"That's too bad," Eddie said. "I thought maybe if I stayed around awhile I'd find out the real answer for you to the mystery of your ugly friend. You don't really believe all that stuff about the message, do you? You don't think your father would go to all that trouble to send you words about being happy?"

"Don't be impertinent," Miss Althea told him. "My father was an unusual man. You never had the good fortune to know him, and I doubt if you would understand his motives."

"Born too late, I guess," Eddie said.

Miss Althea closed her eyes for a moment and Jan moved close to her, fearful lest this encounter make her really ill.

Even Patrick was impatient with his brother now. "Get your duffel bag and come along," he said abruptly. "I know where you can get a room. You shouldn't disturb Mrs. Pendleton like this."

Miss Althea opened her eyes. "Yes, Eddie. I'd like you to leave the house at once. I cannot cope with having

you on the premises. But I want to speak to you alone
first. Run along, children — all of you. The interview is
over."

Neil had been moving idly about the room, pretending
a lack of interest in what went on. He picked up his
equipment and gave Eddie a look of extreme dislike.
Eddie merely grinned at him as if he were hardly worth
staying angry with.

When Neil went out, Patrick followed reluctantly and
Jan went downstairs after the two boys. She did not like
to leave Miss Althea alone with Eddie, but the old lady
seemed to have come through the last hour well, so perhaps he would not upset her.

In the yard Patrick waited in the driveway for his
brother to come down. Neil set his recorder and flight
bag on the ground and waited too. In spite of the way he
had pretended a lack of interest, he did not want to miss
anything. Neither boy spoke to the other.

"Do you know where Eddie will be working at the
Seaport?" Jan asked Patrick.

All the chips seemed to be back on Patrick's shoulder.
He sounded more pugnacious than ever as he answered.

"He's going to help out with tourists aboard the old
whaling ship at the Seaport. Answering questions and
that sort of thing. He knows a lot about ships, so it should
work out fine." But Patrick's look said more than his
words. It expressed his worry about Eddie, his uncertainty
as to whether anything at all would turn out well for his
brother, and that made him all the more defensive.

"Perhaps it will be all right," Jan said, feeling unexpectedly sorry for Patrick Marshall. For the first time
she had been able to see past the guard he held against
the world.

Patrick did not answer, however. His manner showed

clearly that he wanted no sympathy from anyone.

At that moment Eddie came out of the house with his duffel bag on his shoulder and Patrick turned to him eagerly. "Is Mrs. Pendleton all right?" he asked. "You shouldn't have talked to her like that, you know."

His brother spoke carelessly. "She's O.K., I guess. She didn't have much to say. Only the usual lecture about yesterday making today — all that stuff about doing better. She gave up when she saw I wasn't listening and went to lie down. My bag was packed, so I got it and came downstairs. I think the old lady's getting senile."

"Oh, no!" Jan cried indignantly and for once was grateful to Patrick for siding with her.

"If you think that, maybe you're not so bright yourself," he snapped at his brother.

Eddie looked hurt. "So now my kid brother is turning against me too."

Patrick started grimly toward the dock and after a moment's hesitation, Eddie followed him.

Neil looked speculatively after them. "For all your great-grandmother knows, Eddie could have got away with half her jade collection," he said. "I sure wouldn't trust that guy around the house. It's a good thing she got rid of him." He did not wait for Jan's response, but hurried off toward his own house.

˙ Jan walked slowly down to the dock. The little boat was already darting across the river. From the direction of the Kents' house came the sound of Miss Althea's voice, startling her, until she realized that Neil must be playing back his tape recording. Ordinarily, she would have hurried to join him, interested in hearing her own voice on tape, as well as listening to the interview. But all such eagerness had gone out of her. She had an unsettled feeling that she could not place.

Wanting only to be by herself, she walked along the dock and sat cross-legged on gray, sun-heated boards. It was a very warm morning and she would have been more comfortable in the shade, but somehow she wanted to soak up as much sunshine as she could because of the strange, uneasy chill deep inside her.

With all her being she felt that something was wrong. In spite of the fact that the interview had seemed to go well — even though her own part had fallen flat — she had the feeling of an undercurrent that was terribly wrong. It was as if at any moment something dreadful might happen that would cause a lot of trouble and unhappiness, both to herself and to her great-grandmother. What sort of trouble she did not know, but she had the curious feeling that she was the only person in the world who had glimpsed the shadow of some dreadful thing that no one else suspected. What had Eddie said about the mystery not yet being solved? Was there really something wicked about the Chinese image?

She closed her eyes against the dazzle of sunlight on blue water and gave herself a good talking-to. There she went — building fantasies again. She was as bad as Neil. Mom had said to stay away from wild ideas and keep out of trouble.

Reminding herself of this did no good. How could she keep out of trouble when she could not tell in which direction trouble lay? She had the feeling that trouble might spring upon her without warning and bring disaster down upon her head. So strong was this sensation, and so persistent was it, that it finally spurred her to frightened action.

She jumped up and ran all the way back to the Pendleton house. She tore upstairs and into her great-grandmother's living room, half expecting to find that something awful had occurred. Miss Althea, however, was resting quietly on her bed, and the golden scales of a wriggling dragon safely hid the glare of the Chinese image.

Nothing was wrong. Of course nothing was wrong!

13 THE JADE KWAN YIN

SPECULATION WAS ONCE more astir at the back of Jan's mind. Make-believe that went nowhere was purposeless now. However, using her imagination to solve a puzzle was something else. Eddie's feeling that there was more to the mystery than anyone suspected had somehow impressed her.

Perhaps Miss Althea had lived with the puzzle so long that she had given up trying any new approach to a solution. She had long ago accepted what she believed to be the answer. But what if Eddie was right and there was something more? Not about the image itself, but about the words Great-great-grandfather Gillespie Osborn had impressed into the clay of the base. If he had used a sort of code when he put down "Rose of Sharon" to mean Althea, might not the rest be a code as well?

Jan began to feel excited. In spite of herself she was making believe again. She could imagine herself confounding all of them — Miss Althea, Neil, Patrick, and even the unpleasant Eddie — by calmly producing a final answer to the reason why Miss Althea's father had sent the image to her for safekeeping.

If she could produce such an answer, she would undoubtedly bring her great-grandmother much joy. She would also win her approval, so that in spite of any trouble she might get into, Miss Althea would approve of Janice Pendleton and want her to stay. There would be no more worry about being sent away to some distant school where she would have no family at all.

First she would have to stop dreaming and do something practical. Where could she begin? Where could she find the meaning of words that might have been used in a code? She wandered to the bookcase where the name book was kept and looked at the neighboring volumes. One of them was a fat book called a thesaurus. In its columns were given, not definitions, but groups of words that had similar meanings. If you could not think of the exact word you wanted to use, you could look up the nearest word that came to mind, and then track down the right word, the perfect word for the purpose. What if the words "happy" and "heart" carried some other meaning than Miss Althea had guessed?

Jan seated herself on the floor in front of the bookcase and began running through the index. A slip of blank paper lay between the pages, and on a nearby shelf was a china holder of pencils. When she had looked up the word "heart," Jan reached for a pencil and jotted down random words on the paper: essence, substance, vitals, center, meat, inmost mind. There were dozens more, but these were enough "heart" words to start with.

Next she looked up "happy," and again she chose words at random that seemed related to happiness: timely, auspicious, overjoyed, cheerful, blissful, gay, blessed.

None of the words on the two lists seemed to speak to her imagination in any way. Next she tried putting choices from the two groups together in pairs. Blissful vitals, blessed meat, cheerful essence, auspicious inmost mind.

The combinations were so silly and meaningless that she began to smile to herself over them. At least they had cheered her up a little, though she was as far as ever from an answer. She had just put the book back on its shelf when she heard a noise toward the front of the room. It was surely the sound of someone opening a window, but there was no one else in the room with her.

She turned about in her place on the floor so that she could look toward the porch windows, peering around a chair in front of her. One of the windows that had no screen was indeed open. Through it an arm had reached and the hand was about to pick up the precious jade figure of Kwan Yin.

"Don't touch that!" Jan cried, jumping to her feet. The hand and arm vanished at once, leaving Kwan Yin on the table. She heard the sound of someone running across the porch, dashing heavily down the outside stairs, making no attempt now at concealment. She would have run out on the porch to the stairs herself to see who it was, but Miss Althea had heard her cry out and was calling her anxiously from the bedroom. There was such alarm in her tone that Jan dared not leave her call unanswered.

She went quickly to the door and found Miss Althea sitting up in bed.

"What's happened?" the old lady demanded. "Why did you shout like that?"

Jan's words tumbled in her hurry. "Someone just tried to take the—the jade Kwan Yin! If—if I hurry, I can s-s-see who it was."

She turned toward the door, but Miss Althea stopped her. "No—wait! You must be mistaken, Janice. No one has taken the little Kwan Yin. It isn't possible."

"He didn't take it," Jan tried to explain. "I saw the hand and shouted in time. Kwan Yin is there on the table, but whoever it was ran away."

"Come help me, child," Miss Althea said.

There was no escape and Jan offered her arm to help Miss Althea up. She handed her the canes, and then there was a long, slow advance into the other room, with Miss Althea using one cane and gripping Jan's arm tightly with her other hand.

By this time whoever the thief was would be long out of sight, Jan thought helplessly, and gave her full attention to assisting the old lady.

Kwan Yin awaited them on the table's edge. When Miss Althea reached the table, she loosed her great-granddaughter's arm and picked up the little jade figure. Then, to Jan's astonishment and distress, she burst into tears. With Jan's help she reached a nearby chair and sat there weakly, tears running down her cheeks, while the jade Kwan Yin lay in her lap.

Jan remembered the bronze gongs Miss Althea used when she wanted Gran or Mrs. Marshall to come upstairs. She hurried to where they hung — hollow cups strung upon a silken rope — and picked up the padded stick. She bonged lustily on the lower gong and heard the sound go reverberating through the house. Miss Althea did not stir, but went right on weeping.

In a moment Mrs. Marshall came rushing upstairs to inquire what was wrong. Jan explained what had happened, and for a moment she was afraid that Patrick's mother was going to burst into tears too. But Mrs. Marshall managed to control her own fears as she brought Miss Althea a glass of water and a white pill.

"This interview should never have been suggested," Mrs. Marshall said, regarding Jan unhappily. "We knew it would cause trouble. We knew it would upset her."

Jan listened guiltily. The disaster she had feared seemed to have fallen, and though she had been able to stop the actual theft of Kwan Yin, blame was somehow descending like a smothering blanket upon her own head.

When she was sure she was no longer needed, Jan went downstairs and out on the front porch. She saw at once that Patrick's boat was once more tied up at the little dock, but only Patrick and Eddie's duffel bag were in it. Had Patrick taken his brother across to the other side and returned? Or was Eddie lurking somewhere around on this side — after trying to steal Kawn Yin?

As she came down the porch steps, Jan watched the boy in the boat. The arm that had come through the window had worn a rolled-up white sleeve. Patrick, who seemed to be having trouble getting the motor started, had one white sleeve rolled up and the other down. She could not remember how Eddie had been dressed. Neil, as she recalled, had worn his green-checked shirt that morning.

A voice hailed her as she started for the dock, and she looked about to see Neil waving to her from in front of his house. He was indeed wearing the green shirt and it had short sleeves. Anyway, she had not thought it likely that he would be after the jade figure. She changed her course and crossed the driveway between the two houses. Neil came to meet her.

"What's going on?" he asked. "What's the matter with Pat Marshall?"

"What do you mean?" Jan had the feeling that she wanted to postpone whatever Neil was about to tell her.

"Why did he come racing down your outside stairs just now? He looked as if somebody was chasing him for sure!"

"I—I don't know," Jan faltered. "I didn't see him run down the stairs."

"You never do see what's going on over there, do you?" said Neil scornfully.

Jan did not defend herself. "I think I'll go talk to him," she said, and turned quickly away, hoping that Neil would not decide to come with her.

Fortunately, his mother called him for lunch and he went inside and left Jan to go down to the dock alone. Patrick was still fiddling with the motor, and she hurried lest he shove off before she could reach him. He was so preoccupied with what he was doing that he did not see her approach. The motor started with a roar as she reached the dock and without pausing to make up her mind, Jan climbed into the boat.

Patrick scowled at her as they headed out upon the water. His red hair seemed afire in the bright light, and his face was flushed, as it had been earlier.

"What do you want?" he shouted above the roar.

"Why did you try to take the jade lady?" she shouted back.

Patrick did not answer. He steered for the middle of the river, going at a fast clip. Jan hung onto the seat, bracing herself against the vibration of the prow against the water as the boat sped up the river. She had no idea where Patrick was taking her and she certainly did not want to go. There was nothing to do but hang on desperately and hope that Neil had seen them leave before he went into the house. Probably he wouldn't do anything anyway. He wouldn't know that she was, in a sense, be-

ing kidnapped. Once Eddie's duffel bag rolled against her foot, and she shoved it away and raised her voice to ask where they were going. But Patrick, if he heard, did not answer, and she did not try again. The duffel bag had reminded her of Eddie, and she wondered where he was and what he might be doing.

The boat was following the shoreline, nosing in toward an empty section of land well above the row of captains' houses. There was no road here, and a huge mass of rock rose upward from the water's edge toward the woods above. Patrick cut the motor and steered toward a pebbly ledge. He did not go all the way in to shore, or Jan would have jumped out of the boat and run away. She was growing increasingly afraid of this scowling, red-faced boy at the tiller.

They drifted in silence, close to the empty shore, and what houses were in sight seemed all too far away. Patrick began to speak in a low, furious tone.

"What did you tell Mrs. Pendleton?" he demanded.

Jan held tightly to the sides of the boat. "Why — that — that somebody tried to take Kwan Yin. I didn't know it was you."

Patrick snorted, but he looked anxious as well as angry. "What did she say to that?"

"Nothing. She started to cry. When your mother came, I ran outside. Neil said he saw you dashing down the stairs. So I hurried down to the boat to find out what you were up to."

"What I do is none of your business," Patrick snapped. "You're a meddler — that's all. Why can't you tend to your own affairs?"

"So you're a thief too," Jan said, and then could have bitten her tongue. "Too" meant like his brother Eddie.

Patrick looked as though he would like to dump her overboard and let her swim for shore.

"What if I am?" he said grimly. "Everybody is saying we Marshalls are no good. What difference does it make?"

Jan opened her mouth to protest, but he went right on.

"If you want to stay out of trouble — and I mean *trouble* — you'd better keep your mouth shut about this. Act as though you'd never talked to me. Act as though you don't know who that arm you saw belonged to. If you don't — " He left the rest in the air, but a threat was clear.

She could hardly bear to meet his furious eyes, to face him when he looked like this. She had a feeling that he might very well dump her overboard if she angered him enough. Something was at stake here, though she wasn't sure exactly what, and she hung onto the seat, ready to resist if he reached out for her, but determined to have her say.

"If I d-d-don't keep still — then what?" she demanded, hating the way her teeth had a tendency to chatter, as if the day were cold.

"You may get into a whole lot more trouble than you want," Patrick said. "You may get hurt — bad." He started the motor again and ran the nose of the boat onto the pebbly sand of the little ledge. "Get out!" he said. "You can walk home from here."

She didn't dare argue, but neither did she make any promise to keep still. She simply crawled out of the boat and ran up to a path that wound along the shore. She did not look back when the motor started and the boat went off across the water. All she wanted was the safety and reassurance of Gran's house.

It wasn't a long walk home, but it was after lunchtime when she arrived. That did not matter, however, because lunch itself was late. Gran's car stood in the driveway and Gran and Mrs. Marshall were with Miss Althea. Jan went hesitantly upstairs and found that she had not been missed. The moment she appeared, however, Gran gave her a long look and took her downstairs out of Miss Althea's hearing.

From what Gran said, Jan gathered that the old lady had told an astonishing story in her absence. She had said that her great-granddaughter was imagining things again and had believed that someone reached through a window to take the jade lady. Of course this could not have happened in broad daylight. Nevertheless, Miss Althea was upset by Jan's notions and she thought Jan had better stay away from her for a little while — either in her room or downstairs. She did not want to hear any more such alarming talk.

Jan had never seen her cheerful, good-natured grandmother look so stern and unsmiling as when they sat facing each other on the living room couch downstairs. Jan had a dreadful sense of being abandoned, first by Miss Althea, and also by her usually sweet-tempered grandmother.

"I'm afraid that having you in that upstairs room has not worked out," Gran said. "You seem to have been a disturbing influence ever since we moved you up there. I don't suppose you can help this. You are young and you have a need for action and excitement. You've stirred up that old mystery of the Chinese image as well, and this sort of thing can make Mother ill. You don't realize how old she is, or how quiet we must keep her."

Jan felt she had to answer that, whether Gran liked

it or not. "I don't think Miss Althea wants to be quiet. Dad said—"

"Your father is on the other side of the world and can't possibly know what is going on here," Gran continued firmly. "Everything has been in a state of turmoil since you moved upstairs. I didn't think it would work out, because of course a young person brings other young people around. I couldn't approve of this taped interview —and I was right. It has all proved much too upsetting for Mother."

"But she liked talking about China," Jan protested. "She enjoyed—"

"I hope you aren't the sort of child who likes to argue," Gran said. "I'm beginning to feel quite upset myself. You must understand that we cannot have any more trouble in this house. At the next sign of a problem, we will have to move you downstairs, though that means you won't have a room of your own. Perhaps the only solution is the one your parents suggested if things don't work out here. That is, to arrange for you to go to school in Boston for a year or two until your family returns to the States."

Miss Minchin's! Jan thought, and blinked hard to hold back her tears. Everything was cracking up around her, yet somehow she could not help but feel that this time she was right and Gran was wrong, though there was nothing she could do or say in her own defense.

Her grandmother relented then and touched her cheek with a gentle hand. "I'm sorry, dear. We all hoped this would work out—for Mother's sake as well as for yours. What do you say we try again? Do you think you can promise me that there will be no more trouble? No more upsets for your great-grandmother? No more excursions on the part of that vivid imagination of yours?"

Jan opened her mouth to answer, then closed it again and nodded miserably. "I'll try," she mumbled. Gran patted her cheek again and went to help Mrs. Marshall get lunch.

Jan sat alone on the couch, fighting her tears. Homesickness was back in a terrible, smothering wave. For a while she had been happy and busy and interested and she hadn't thought so much about needing her family. Now all she wanted was Mom's arms about her so she could pour out the whole miserable story to ears that would understand and believe — as she knew Mom would believe. She wanted to be comforted.

How could it have been her fault that Patrick Marshall had crept upstairs and tried to steal the little jade figure? Yet she could not tell Mrs. Marshall or Gran that he had been the one. Not after the threat he had made. Perhaps they wouldn't believe her anyway after the things Miss Althea had said. That was the worst part of it all — the feeling that Miss Althea had somehow betrayed her.

"Come to lunch, dear," Gran called.

Jan rose and went dully to the table. She was not at all hungry. She did not think she would ever be hungry again. The cheese omelet tasted like sawdust and she could hardly swallow.

14 A BRASS JAR

THE NEXT FEW days were hard to get through. Two airmail letters arrived from Mom and Dad, but they only increased Jan's feeling of standing alone against the world. She read them over and over, and when she was by herself in the room that was still hers, she wept over them, no longer trying to be brave.

At least she kept out of trouble. She avoided Miss Althea as far as possible, and when she glimpsed the old lady it seemed to Jan that her great-grandmother was relieved not to talk to her. They were no longer friends. Neither Patrick nor Eddie came around, as far as she knew. Once or twice she saw Neil from a distance, but she stayed away from him too, lest he ask questions about Patrick and that boat ride she had taken.

Only her thoughts would not stay out of trouble. Sometimes she grew angry over the injustice that had been dealt her. Sometimes she was merely sorry for herself. And there were other times when her thoughts went darting off wildly, making up stories in which she was the misjudged heroine who was at last vindicated because she stepped in to reveal the truth of all that had happened. In these daydreams, she could imagine Eddie stealing up the outside stairs, intending to do Miss Althea harm, only to have Janice Pendleton block and defeat him, showing him up for the evildoer he was.

Whatever direction her imaginings might take, the ugly Chinese image seemed to glare through them, staring at her with his pop eyes — trying to tell her something. Again and again she went over the words she had looked up in the thesaurus, but without further result. She even added more words to her collection, but none of them made any sense and she knew she was no closer to the answer than before.

Just one new idea came to her. She had been focusing upon only two words of the message: "happy" and "heart." There was a third word that she had overlooked: "find." This she did not need to look up for its meanings. She knew well enough what the substitute words for "find" might be. She thought of "discover" and "unearth" and "reveal." This was the word of direction in the message, the word of command, and it began to seem more and more important as she thought about it.

Why had "Rose of Sharon" been directed to *find* a happy heart? There seemed to be some sort of search implied, but there was nothing to search. She had examined the Chinese image carefully and it had given neither her nor anyone else who had looked at it in the past, any particular clue. So *where* was one supposed to search? In what other possessions of her great-grandmother's? Althea Osborn Pendleton had decided that it was her own heart which must be searched. Janice Pendleton, who was the great-great-granddaughter of Gillespie Osborn, kept wondering if this was so.

So strong did the question become in her mind that she finally decided that she must have one more look at

the image. It still sat in Miss Althea's living room, covered with the gold and black satin square on which the
dragon rippled its scales. The jade Kwan Yin had been
returned to the cabinet but no one had moved the Chinese
image. Since it spelled trouble to Jan, she had avoided it
to the extent of giving it a very wide berth when she so
much as walked through the room. But the question in
her mind would not be quiet, and on this particular rainy
morning she decided that she must look at the figure
again.

Miss Althea was lying down for her midmorning nap.
Jan made sure of that, listening near her door for the
light, rhythmic breathing that reassured her. Gran was
at the bookstore over in the Seaport, and Mrs. Marshall
was running a vacuum cleaner downstairs. The coast was
as clear as it would ever be. Boldly Jan went to the desk
where the image sat and jerked off the square of satin.

She stood staring in horrified disbelief. No ugly,
goggling face looked back at her. No fangs snarled in a
frightening smile. In the place where the image had sat
stood a squat brass jar with fat sides that approximated
the shape of the Chinese image. She stood looking helplessly from the piece of satin in her hands to the shiny
jar. From the bedroom there seemed a slight change in
Miss Althea's breathing. Hurriedly Jan flung the cloth
over the vase and stepped away from it. But her great-
grandmother still slept, and after a moment of listening,
Jan dropped to her hands and knees and crawled about
the floor, looking futilely under the desk, under chairs —
everywhere. The image was nowhere around. Not under
anything, nor in, nor on anything.

Someone had removed it and left the jar in its place,
clearly intending to fool Miss Althea into thinking the

Chinese image was under the cloth.

Jan went to her room and closed the door. This was dreadful. This was the worst kind of trouble possible. If Miss Althea discovered her loss, she would be upset all over again. She might not like the old thing, but she wanted it around. It was a part of her life, and Jan knew very well that its loss would distress her a very great deal. What was more, Jan herself might well be blamed for its disappearance. After all, she had taken it from its place twice. She had put it back both times, but her interest in the Chinese image and her curiosity about it were well known. Eddie was gone from the house and surely could not have come back at night to take it without Jan waking to hear him.

She began to wonder exactly when the image had been taken. She had been thinking in terms of a theft in the last day or two. But perhaps Patrick could have taken the image at the same time that he tried to take Kwan Yin. The desk was not far from the window. But no — surely it had been the opening of the window Jan had heard that had made her turn around. Patrick had not come into the room at all, as far as she knew. He could have done nothing more than reach for the jade lady before Jan stopped him.

Suddenly she knew exactly how it must have happened. The person who had always been most interested in the image was Eddie Marshall. He had been on the tower stairs when Miss Althea had instructed Jan to cover the figure from view — so he knew where it was. Then she had sent the children from the house so that she could talk to Eddie alone. Later he had come outside, carrying his duffel bag, and he had said Mrs. Pendleton had gone to her bedroom to lie down. He had carried that bag down to his brother's boat. It had been in the boat when Patrick had taken Jan upriver. She remembered how it had rolled against her foot, so that she had kicked it away. If only she had opened it at the time, she might have seen the image grinning out at her. Eddie would have had no trouble at all about picking it up and substituting the jar before he left the house.

What was to be done? Somehow, somehow, Jan must find out where the figure was and recover it before Miss Althea knew it was missing. Finding it was up to her. There was no one else to keep this final disaster from falling. Nevertheless, she needed to consult someone, to get help in her effort. She looked out the window to find that the rain had lessened for the moment and she put on a slicker and rain hood and went over to Neil's house.

Mrs. Kent answered the doorbell and said Neil was on the sun porch playing one of his interview tapes. Jan went in to join him and found that he was once more playing the interview with Miss Althea. She stopped in surprise to listen to her own voice.

Neil grinned at her. "Hi! Yes—that's you. Nobody sounds the way he thinks he should on tape," he assured her. "I thought you'd come over before this to hear it. It turned out pretty well, considering all the interruptions."

She could not explain that she had felt so resentful over being misjudged that she had not wanted to hear the tape. Nor had she wanted to face any questions from Neil. Now she did not care.

"I had to talk to you," she told him.

At her sober tone he turned off the recorder. "Something's happened?"

She nodded. "The Chinese image is gone."

"What do you mean—gone?" Neil stared at her. "Gone where?"

She told him the whole story—how she had caught Patrick Marshall trying to steal Kwan Yin, and the details of her talk with him in the boat, even repeating his warning to mind her own business if she did not want to get hurt. She told him as well of the trouble she was in at home, and about Eddie's duffel bag and the fact that she suspected the image had been in it when he left the house.

Neil listened, his eyes bright with excitement. Once he broke into her flow of words. "Hey—wait a minute! This is good. Let me get it down on tape."

Jan made a face at him. "If you try to put me on tape, I won't say another word. This isn't an interview. I only wanted to talk to someone who could help me figure out what to do."

"O.K.— if that's what you want," Neil said cheerfully. "Go ahead and tell me the rest."

Jan hesitated, remembering that Neil had a grudge against both Patrick and Eddie Marshall, and might be all too willing to give out advice that would get them into trouble. Nevertheless, there was no one else to whom she could turn, so she went on and finished the story of how she had kept to herself and stayed safely out of trouble for several days. Then this morning she had started thinking about the mystery again, trying to figure it out—and when she had decided to look at the image, she had found it missing, with a brass jar set in its place.

Neil looked positively pleased over the news, as if anything that might further involve Patrick and Eddie was something he could enjoy. But when it came to figur-

ing out what to do next, or how to get the figure back, he had no immediate suggestion.

"Maybe I could go over to the Seaport and talk to Eddie's grandfather again," Jan said, thinking aloud. "He was friendly the other time I saw him. He doesn't approve of Eddie, so he might help me get the image back."

"I don't know about that." Neil sounded doubtful. "Wouldn't it be better to talk to Eddie himself? He's working every day over at the whaling ship. I've seen him there. If you talk to his grandfather first, Eddie may get his wind up and know you're suspicious of him. Then you'll never find the thing at all."

"I still think his grandfather might help me," Jan insisted. "He won't want any more scandal about Eddie, and he's very fond of Patrick. All I need to do is get the image returned before Miss Althea knows it's gone. If she doesn't know, maybe I can stay out of trouble awhile longer. I don't care about who took it or why — so long as it comes back."

Neil's eyes had the same bright, inventive look that Jan had seen in them once or twice before — as though ideas were beginning to crowd one another in his mind. It occurred to her that she and Neil were a little alike in this and the fact made her uneasy about any plans he might concoct.

His next words took a surprising turn. "Do you think you have the right to protect someone who is trying to steal things? What if Eddie put Pat up to taking the Kwan Yin so he could sell it and get a lot of money? Pat would do about anything for his brother. I guess Eddie really belongs in jail and if you keep quiet about all this, you'll only help him get away with it."

What Neil said might be true, but she had to remember that he might be guided by his own wish to punish those who had humiliated him. Advice that was so prejudiced might not be worth taking. In spite of everything, she did not want to see Eddie sent back to jail, or to see Patrick get into a lot of trouble. There must be some other way to handle this and still make Eddie and Patrick realize their own wrongdoing.

"I'm going to talk to Grandpa Marshall," she decided. "I'll go see him right after lunch. Gran will drive me to the Seaport when she goes back to the bookstore."

Neil continued to look doubtful. "Are you sure you've told me everything? Or are you holding something important back?"

The only thing she had held back was her own wish not to get anyone into more trouble. And she did not know whether this feeling was justified. Anyway, she wanted no more discussion with Neil. The way he watched her with that bright look in his eyes made Jan remember what his mother had said about his making up stories in his head and trying to act them out. If he mixed himself up in this, things might be tangled for sure.

"I only needed you to talk to," she told him. "I think I've figured out what to do. So don't *you* do anything!"

He grinned at her. "At least I'll wait till you've had your talk with Grandpa Marshall. If you don't have any better ideas, maybe I can help. I could talk to my dad."

Jan had heard enough. "Don't do that! Not yet. It's our affair—not his."

Neil shrugged. "O.K. If that's how you feel. Let me know what's happened when you get back this afternoon. Would you like me to come along when you go over to the Seaport?"

She shook her head vigorously, very sure that she did not want Neil along. To satisfy him she promised that she would come over to see him as soon as she got home. Then she returned to the house and waited impatiently for lunchtime, on pins and needles lest someone happened to look underneath that square of black satin, to discover the dreadful truth. Tomorrow, she recalled, was Mrs. Marshall's day for a thorough dusting of Miss Althea's rooms. That made everything that much more urgent. Tomorrow, without any doubt, the secret would be learned. The real trouble would begin.

After lunch Gran accepted without comment her wish to go to the Seaport in spite of the rainy day. She had been very kind and considerate ever since their talk, but Jan did not feel at all reassured. She knew how much she wanted to stay in Mystic while her parents were away. And she wanted Miss Althea for her friend again. If she could recover the image and solve the mystery that Eddie too must be after, then everyone would be pleased. She would feel at home again, and Miss Althea would approve of her. On the other hand, it would be awful if Gran wrote Mom and Dad that Jan was too much trouble for two old ladies to have around, so they could not keep her with them any longer.

This must never happen! She had only this afternoon to find an answer, and, as she had told Neil, she would start with Grandpa Marshall. He was carving a model of the *Happy Heart* for Miss Althea. He would not want to see her hurt, and he would want to make sure that his own grandsons stayed out of trouble.

15 ROPE WALK

IT WAS RAINING quite hard by the time she arrived at the Seaport with Gran. No cars were allowed inside, so they parked in the area across the road from the entrance and hurried through the gate. Jan wore her slicker and rain hood and rubber boots. She left Gran at the bookstore and hurried along the waterfront street. Not many people were about today and the river looked gray and smooth under pelting rain.

As she passed the plank wharf where the old whaling ship was moored, she saw its bowsprit extending landward, with masts, empty of sails, rising skyward. Eddie Marshall was nowhere in sight. Probably he was on deck under shelter, well out of the rain.

She skirted a huge ship's anchor, set upon the waterfront as a display, and hurried toward the low gray building of the rope walk. Rain clattered on her hood and slicker and she was streaming rivulets by the time she ran up the steps to the door and entered the dim interior.

Other rain-soaked visitors had obviously dripped across the wooden floor, since there were wet patches near the door. The place was very quiet except for the sound of rain beating on the pitched roof overhead. For a moment she thought no one was there. Then she saw Grandpa Marshall sitting on a wooden barrel with the model of the sailboat, *Happy Heart,* on a ledge before him. He had brought it down from the loft, and she saw that he was lettering a white card with great care, now and then pausing to prop it up against the model.

When she had watched him for a few moments he looked around and smiled at her, but she knew he did not remember who she was until she took off her hood and held it dripping away from her head.

"You're Janice, aren't you?" he said. "Mrs. Pendleton's great-granddaughter."

She nodded, suddenly tongue-tied, now that she was here. How was she to begin talking about Eddie and Patrick?

"You've kept the secret, I hope," he went on. "I mean about my little sailing craft here. I've finished work on it and I mean to take it over to Mrs. Pendleton when I go out for lunch. I'm finishing up a card to go with it."

"I haven't told," Jan said. This, at least, was a safe subject, and she stepped nearer to admire the graceful little boat.

"Patrick was around a few minutes ago," the old man continued, working carefully with his inking pen. "You just missed him."

Jan was glad of that. Patrick was the last person she wanted to see. First she must get a few things straight, but before she could sort out her thoughts and decide on a good way to begin, Grandpa Marshall spoke again.

"The boy had a story to tell me," he said, setting the card on the deck of the *Happy Heart* and regarding it gravely. "Maybe the rest of us have been wrong about Eddie. I've heard about the trouble he got into a few days ago up at your place. All the same, maybe Patrick is right and we haven't been as generous as we should be."

Jan waited, not sure what he meant. The old man looked at her almost sternly beneath shaggy gray eyebrows and nodded his head.

"I've decided that I'm going to give Eddie the benefit of the doubt for a change. I'm going to give him a chance to prove that he means to change so that things will be different now. After all, I've got to give the boy credit for coming back to Mystic to face up to everyone who knew he was in trouble."

Jan listened in dismay. She did not believe that Eddie had changed, but what Grandpa Marshall had said made it impossible for her to tell him that Eddie was already in a lot of new trouble.

Quietly the old man continued. "Eddie has told Patrick that he wasn't involved in the holdup in New York that he went to jail for. He admits running with the wrong crowd. But he claims that he left those two fellows that night and that he wanted nothing to do with what they planned. They were sore because he walked out on them, so when they were caught they implicated him as well."

Patrick had tried to tell Miss Althea this, Jan remembered, but she had not believed it. She had pointed out sadly that there had been a trial, that she had helped to pay for a good lawyer, but that Eddie had been found guilty.

"Weren't there witnesses who identified Eddie?" Jan asked hesitantly.

"Witnesses have been wrong before," the old man said. "When there's a lot of excitement people can get mixed up about what they think they've seen."

Jan was silent. Her heart felt heavy with pity. Not for Eddie, but for his grandfather. She could not possibly tell him now about the taking of the Chinese image, or about how Patrick had tried to steal Kwan Yin and had actually threatened Jan if she told about what he had done. For a moment she almost wished Neil were here because she suspected that he would not hesitate because of Grandpa Marshall's feelings. Neil would burst right into whatever needed to be said. But he wasn't here and she knew she could not add to the load of worry Eddie's grandfather was carrying.

The old man must have become aware of the doubts expressed by her silence, for he went on gently, kindly. "Maybe the important thing isn't what Eddie did or didn't do in the past. Maybe the only way we can judge anyone fairly is by present behavior. Patrick thinks Eddie has changed."

Patrick was busy trying to help his brother at all costs, Jan thought, but she could not say so.

"Where did Patrick go?" she asked when the silence grew long.

"I haven't a notion." Grandpa Marshall shook the card a few times to dry the lettering and gave the sailboat a last pat of approval. "I've been working around in different places all morning. Didn't even see him leave. Just came along to the front door and saw he was gone."

She didn't really want to know where Patrick was, Jan thought, since she did not care to run into him herself. A thought at the back of her mind was growing stronger all the time, urging her to take action she did not want to take.

"I'm leaving now," Grandpa Marshall said and got into his oilskins. He picked up the sailboat under one

arm and started for the door. "I'll drive over to Mrs. Pendleton's and leave this for her. If you want to stay here
and look around, it's all right. This place doesn't need
to be locked up in the middle of the day. There's nothing
here for anyone to disturb." Before Jan could think of
anything further to say, he had picked up an umbrella
and gone out the front door.

The rain had let up a little so that the drumming on the
roof had lessened. There was a rushing sound of water
in drains, the dripping from eaves, and from tree branches
outside, but inside the rope walk everything seemed very
still and dark. There were a few electric bulbs here and
there, but with no sunlight to throw bright squares along
the far stretch of the walk the building seemed to run like
a dark tunnel toward the rear door, closed today against
the rain. The effect was somehow eerie, yet Jan did not
leave at once. Because of the utter quiet, this was a place
in which she could think without interruption. Goodness
only knew, she certainly needed to think. And there was
nothing here to be afraid of.

Idly she left the front section with the open loft above,
and started down the long walk. Some of the windows
were closed today, and the smell of dust and hemp and
ancient wood was thick on the air. Once she sneezed as
she walked along, and right afterwards she seemed to
hear a creaking of wood high above and toward the
front, almost echoing her sneeze. She stood still for a
moment, listening, but there was no further sound.

The urgency at the back of her mind was becoming
more insistent. There was just one person she must
bring herself to talk to. Whether she liked it or not, she
would have to do as Neil had suggested and see Eddie
Marshall. She would have to tell him that she knew what
he had done and that if he did not give her the image to

put back in its place, she would have to tell Mrs. Pendleton the truth. Her very skin prickled with goose bumps at the thought of such action. But what else was there to do? Neil was no help. He would do everything according to his own notions, whether what he believed was right or wrong. And Patrick was against her and warning her not to meddle. She would not consult Grandpa Marshall, and she could imagine the trouble that might break out if she told Gran. No—the image must be safely back in its place before disaster could fall again.

She turned toward the front of the building and this time as she followed the long corridor, she looked up toward the overhead loft where the spinning wheel stood. The sides of the loft were open rails, and as she stared upward in the gloom it seemed as though something moved up there. At once she came to a halt on the walk, her heart drumming in her ears.

"Who—who's there?" she called.

For a moment there was only breathless silence, and then the creaking sound was repeated. The same sound she had heard before. Someone was up there.

Suddenly and clearly a hoarse whisper came to her from the high, gloomy loft: "Go home and mind your own business! Stay out of trouble! Go home, little girl, or you'll get hurt!"

Abruptly fear left her. She knew who was up there and his words made her angry. She had heard them before and she had endured enough of Patrick's threats. He didn't have her out in a boat where she could be dumped overboard this time. Indignantly she moved toward the front section where steep steps led to the loft above. But she had taken no more than a step or two when a block of wood came whizzing through the air in her direction. It barely missed her head and went clattering along the wooden floor of the walk. The next chip struck her lightly on the shoulder, and then a larger piece skimmed her cheek.

She could not stand up to the barrage that was being aimed in her direction. The boy up there in the loft meant to frighten her, even if he had to hurt her in doing so. Alarmed, she turned and raced down the long tunnel of the walk toward the rear door and burst through it, out into the drizzle.

There was mud at the foot of the back steps and along the side of the building, but she ran squishing through it in her boots and did not stop until she was well away from the waterfront street. She ran past the village green and into the winding maze of little houses. Her one thought was to be where there were lights and people and no angry boy who threatened her and flung wood blocks in her direction.

Light in the window of a small frame house caught her attention. The door stood open and through it she could see someone inside. She hurried through the door and stood at the back of what was apparently a school-room, still frightened and breathing heavily. There were rows of gray desks here and an old-fashioned iron stove in the aisle, its long pipe running overhead across the room and disappearing through a hole in the wall. Before the blackboard stood a man in old-fashioned dress and she was about to speak to him when she realized that he was only a dummy figure in the garb of a schoolteacher of last century.

Her breathing quieted. At least no one would look for her here. She sat down on one of the wooden benches and clasped her hands on the desk before her, trying to pretend that she was a pupil in this long-ago school. Some schoolboy had carved a heart into the desk with his penknife and set initials in it, and she traced them with one finger. Who had C. G. and L. O. been?

But she did not really care. She could remember the way a wooden chip had grazed her cheek and she was still frightened. Nevertheless, she knew that as soon as she collected herself, she must go on with what she intended. Patrick or not, she could not run like a rabbit back to Gran's bookstore when she had accomplished exactly nothing. The image was missing and Eddie Marshall must be faced.

A sudden thought came to her. What if she had been wrong in her guess that it was Patrick up there in the loft? Whoever it was had called her a little girl. What if it had been Eddie himself? She had not seen him aboard the ship when she went by, and Grandpa Marshall had been working in different parts of the building, so he would not know if Eddie had come in quietly and gone upstairs to the loft.

The teacher at the front of the schoolroom continued to stand before his blackboard, chalk in hand, the arithmetic problem on the board still unfinished. Jan had the eerie feeling that the black-clothed figure might turn and speak to her at any moment. She jumped up and ran outside again.

This time her feet took her with certainty in the direction of the whaling ship. The rain lessened to a drizzle and then stopped altogether as she followed a side street toward the waterfront. There was a tiny patch of blue showing overhead, so the weather was probably going to clear. Somehow the thought lifted her spirits a little. With the sun shining brightly, the Seaport would be less gloomy and deserted, less like a ghost village out of the past.

The sound of footsteps on the walk behind made her

turn, and she found herself facing Patrick Marshall as he caught up with her. There was no time for her to run. No time to do anything. His expression was grim, his eyes stormy.

"You stay away from my brother!" he said.

She was less afraid of him out here in the open. "You're a fine one to talk!" she cried. "After the way you've behaved! Trying to scare me, threatening me!"

"All I want is for you to leave Eddie alone," he warned.

Jan forgot all caution. "Because you're a thief, just like he is?"

He grabbed her arm and gave her a shake. "What do you mean by that?"

"I caught you stealing Kwan Yin, didn't I? So what else are you but a thief?"

He pushed her from him in disgust. "How stupid can you get! I wasn't stealing that jade figure. I was putting it back."

Jan had turned away, but she whirled around, gaping at him. "Putting it back?"

"Of course, dopey. You're so smart, you think you know it all. That was all I was doing — putting the jade piece back on the table. I was pulling my arm out of the window opening when you started yelping."

Jan stared at him while a number of things suddenly fell into place in her mind. No matter how he behaved, it had been hard for her to believe that Patrick was a thief. So he had been trying to help his brother from the beginning. Even his threats were an effort to conceal Eddie's wrongdoing. Though throwing blocks of wood at her was going too far.

"So it was Eddie," she said. "He must have taken Kwan Yin at the same time that he took the Chinese

image. He could have put them both in his duffel bag
before he left the house."

Patrick blinked at her angrily. "What are you talking
about?"

"About the Chinese image, of course," Jan said.
"The one with the mystery about it. This morning I
looked under that square of satin Miss Althea told me to
put over it — and it was gone. I don't think anyone has
touched it since that day, so Eddie must have taken it at
the same time that he took Kwan Yin."

Patrick looked suddenly frightened as well as angry.
Without another word, he started past Jan in the direction of the ship. She knew he meant to confront his
brother with this new theft and she hurried after him,
intending to hear whatever Eddie had to say.

As they neared the wharf Patrick started to run. She
knew he would like to leave her behind, but this she
would not let him do. They ran together across the wet
cobblestones of the waterfront street and down the wharf
toward the whaling ship. There a boy in a canvas raincoat, perched on a barrel, stopped them.

"Hey — wait a minute!" Neil Kent called.

Jan's heart sank. Neil was the last person she wanted to
have around at this time, but Patrick came to a halt,
eyeing him suspiciously.

Neil grinned at Jan. "You're not so smart, are you?
While you've been running around trying to figure out
what to do, I've found the Chinese image. I know where
Eddie put it. I know where it is right now."

For a moment Jan thought Patrick would hit the other
boy and there would be a fight there on the wharf. She
glanced anxiously up at the ship and saw that Eddie
stood at the rail looking down at them. She could not tell

if he had heard Neil's words.

At the last minute, Patrick managed to control the quick Marshall temper. "O.K.! If you're so smart — show me," he said.

Neil's grin continued to mock them both, but he jumped down from the barrel and started toward the ship. Wooden steps had been built along the side to make it easier for visitors to come aboard the old whaler. As he reached the steps, Neil hailed Eddie up on the deck above.

"Hi there, Cap'n! Is it all right if we come aboard?"

Eddie was watching Neil warily, but he gave him a curt nod, and the three mounted the steps and jumped down to the cleanly sanded decks of the ship. At any other time Jan would have been fascinated by the masts and the ropes and rigging, the great steering wheel in the stern — but now she saw everything in a quick blur.

"Would you like a tour?" Eddie asked. "Maybe the little girl would like to see the try-works where they used to boil the oil out of whale blubber."

"That would be fine," Patrick said. "You take her around, Eddie. Neil wants to show me something."

Jan had no intention of being left on deck with Eddie Marshall. When Neil led the way to an open hatch and started down a ladder, with Patrick following, she did not hesitate. In her haste, she almost stepped on Patrick's hands in order to follow the two boys down. Eddie seemed curious and uneasy, but he did not try to stop them.

Below decks electric lights burned, but the cabin and steerage area seemed dim after the outdoors. Neil wasted no time. He started at once down a second ladderway that descended to the lower hold of the ship. Patrick followed him, and again Jan came after, though it gave her a creepy feeling to go down and down into this closed-in region below the waterline.

At the foot of the ladder a narrow walkway led fore and aft the length of the ship. On each side of it lay piles of rock, used as ballast when there was no cargo. Everything seemed wrapped in a dim, dun-colored gloom. The rocks were dun, and so were the wooden timbers of the ship curving upward on either side. The entire area was interspersed with occasional wooden posts that helped support the structure above. Despite open hatches, the air smelled dead and close down here, and Jan looked longingly at the ladder that led upward to fresh air and the deck two flights above.

But Neil did not linger near the ladder. He was making his way into the stern of the ship. Patrick followed and Jan thumped after him in her rubber boots. It was hot down here where summer warmth had been held in for so long, but there was no time for Jan to get out of her raincoat and boots.

Neil paused on the wooden walk, pointing. "There you are! Come over here and you can see for yourself."

Jan's eyes followed his reaching finger and she gulped in terror. Whitened bones lay upon the rocks. Then she saw the card fastened to a beam above, explaining that these were the skull and bones of a small whale. It was not to these that Neil had pointed. There was something beyond.

Patrick clambered past him onto the rocks and saw what might have looked rather like the rest of the ballast rock unless one searched closely. Grinning out at them from a place far back among the stones was the fang-toothed smile of the Chinese image. Even as Jan saw it,

Patrick reached the figure and bent to pick it up.

"I thought Eddie was acting queerly when I came over here this afternoon," Neil said. "So I kept watch when he didn't know I was around. He had the thing stashed away in the galley at first. When he got it and started down to the hold, I followed him and saw where he hid it. Then I sneaked back upstairs and hung around, waiting for Jan to show up so I could tell her where it was."

Patrick climbed back across the rocks with the figure in his hands. When he reached the walk, Jan reached out and took it from him before he had time to prevent her. Quickly she carried it toward a light to examine it carefully. As she feared, some damage had been done. The old fellow's chin was chipped, and he had been banged against a stone hard enough to break off a bit of the base. When she turned the figure over she found that the word "Rose" was gone from the message on the base. If Miss Althea discovered this, she would not like it at all. But at least the figure had been recovered and all Jan thought of was to get it back to the house where she could replace it beneath the square of black satin.

Behind her, the two boys seemed to be wrangling with each other, but she had no further interest in who was to blame for anything. Carrying the image as if it were a baby cradled in her arms, she started toward the ladder—only to come to a halt on the plank walk. A pair of legs was descending to the lower hold, and as her eyes followed them upward, she saw that Eddie Marshall stood at the foot of the ladder, blocking her way, his eyes upon the Chinese figure that Jan held so tenderly in her arms.

Neil saw him and shouted. "There's your thief! Now we know what he did with the idol when he stole it from Mrs. Pendleton this last time. He was going to hide it down here until he could find out why it was valuable. That's true, isn't it, Eddie? Once a thief, always a thief!"

"My brother's no thief!" Patrick cried and advanced upon Neil.

The other boy backed away, but he kept up his mocking outburst. "Oh, sure — I know all about how Eddie claims he wasn't mixed up in that holdup in New York. But my dad says criminals always swear they're innocent. He says — "

Patrick gave Neil a sudden push that sent him sprawling backward onto the rock pile, but he did not follow up by springing upon him. Instead, he ran down the walkway toward Jan, snatched the image from her arms before she guessed his intention, thrust his way past his surprised brother, and clambered up the ladder.

It was Jan who sensed his purpose and flung herself after him. But Patrick was moving at top speed and she heard his feet running along the deck as she climbed the second ladder and came out into bright sunshine and fresh air. The ship lay at the wharf with its prow pointing landward, its stern toward the river, and already Patrick was leaning over the rail at the stern.

Before Jan could reach him, the dreadful thing was done. Patrick had raised the Chinese figure in his hands and flung it outward into the river. It fell with a great splash as Jan stood beside him, watching in horror the circling ripples that widened and spread out and out, away from the place where the image had vanished beneath the surface of the water.

16 MISS ALTHEA CHOOSES

JAN'S ATTENTION WAS still fixed, as though she were hypnotized, upon the place where idle ripples played across the river, and no mark remained to show what had happened. Beside her, Patrick stared, as spellbound as she, and neither turned when Eddie and Neil came up behind them.

"What did you do that for, kid?" Eddie asked. His tone was surprisingly quiet, his mocking attitude gone.

All the fight had gone out of Patrick. He sounded limp and hopeless as he answered. "I wanted to get rid of it. If there isn't anything to show, nobody can say that you stole it."

"Mrs. Pendleton won't like this," Eddie said. "I don't know how you're going to tell her."

Patrick did not look at his brother. "Anyway, you can't ever steal it again, the way you did Kwan Yin."

Eddie moved quickly. He grabbed Patrick by one shoulder and swung him about. "Then you do know what's happened to the jade piece? I've been scared to death I'd lost it from my bag. Where is it?"

Jan found herself staring at Eddie, just as his brother stared at him.

"I put it back," Patrick said. "Your duffel bag was open when you left it in the boat that time you went to look for a room. When I tried to close it I saw the jade figure inside. So I took it out and put it back on the table in Mrs. Pendleton's room."

For a moment Jan thought Eddie would explode, he looked so furious. But almost at once anger seemed to wash out of him, leaving bitterness behind. There was a bite to his words when he spoke.

"I thought you were the one who was on my side, Pat. I thought you were the one — out of this whole town — who believed I was telling the truth. Old Mrs. Pendleton used to think so. I know she put up the money to pay a lawyer for my defense. When things went wrong, she tried to help me. That's why I came back to Mystic. That's why I wanted to show people that I'd changed from what they thought — so they'd know Mrs. Pendleton was right in trying to give me a chance. But everyone's against me. Even you."

Patrick looked as though he wanted to cry. There was nothing worse, Jan thought, than misjudging someone and finding out later that you had done a lot of harm because you had spoken and acted hastily. At the back of her mind a thought had begun to tap again, as if asking for admission. When she tried to grasp it, the idea eluded her, and she listened again to what Eddie and his brother were saying.

"All the same, you did take the Chinese image the first time, didn't you?" Patrick said.

"Sure. I wanted a good look at the thing. I hadn't seen it since I was a kid. If I could prove that it was valuable in some way, I thought I might repay Mrs. Pendleton for trying to help me by showing her the truth about it."

"But—but what about the jade piece?" Patrick faltered. "Why did you take that?"

"I didn't *take* it. Mrs. Pendleton gave it to me. But I didn't like what she gave it to me for and I was going to return it to her when I'd proved something. She said I'd caused nothing but trouble and she wanted me to leave town. She insisted that I take the jade piece because it would bring me a good deal of money when I sold it. I could go somewhere else and make a new start. She wouldn't hear of my turning her down and she was getting excited. So I took Kwan Yin with me when she insisted, even though I didn't mean to do what she said. I had this job at the Seaport for a starter until I could find something better. And I was going to stay and prove I was as good as anybody else. Then I'd have returned it to her."

Jan was staring at the water again. The persistent idea nagged at the back of her mind and she turned about to locate Neil. Patrick seemed to be swallowing hard and Eddie looked defiant and deeply hurt. Behind them Neil listened with his mouth open in astonishment.

Jan tried to put something into words. "You didn't give anybody much chance to be nice to you," she told Eddie. "You made fun of us and acted as though you had a chip on your shoulder all the time."

"People weren't behaving in a very friendly way toward me," Eddie said. "I couldn't let them know I cared. But I thought my kid brother believed in me, anyway. I thought he was my friend."

Beside Jan, Patrick pounded the rail with his fist and she knew how angry and impatient and desperate he felt—because of his own past actions. She looked at the water again, as though it might help her to focus. The

idea was gathering force in her imagination. Everything
was beginning to click into place. She stood by quietly
and let the whole thing come. Sometimes when you
talked too fast and too soon, an idea would evaporate
at the mere wagging of the tongue. She had to be still
and think about this.

Find a happy heart. Find—to look, to search. And
nobody had looked carefully enough. She remembered
the feeling of the image in her hands, with the piece
broken off one corner. Then, there was the word
"happy"—she knew what that meant, and she knew
what the heart of a thing should be. And now it was too
late to find out whether she was right because the Chinese
image lay at the bottom of the Mystic River.

She turned slowly to face the others, and at that moment the rest of the idea fell completely into place. She
looked at Neil.

"How did you know Eddie claimed to be innocent of
what he went to jail for? How could you know?"

"Everybody knows," Neil protested, blustering a
little. But suddenly a curious thing began to happen. A
slow flood of red moved up into his face clear to his very
forehead—the red of a guilty blushing.

"So it was you up in the loft at the rope walk?" Jan
went on. "You heard what Grandpa Marshall told me,
didn't you? And you were afraid I might come up there
and find you. You didn't want that because you were
planning such a wicked thing. You threw wood chips at
me to scare me away and keep me from finding out it
was you."

Neil was still red, and he had begun to look frightened
as well. "They were only little old chips. They wouldn't
have hurt you." Slowly he began to edge backward

toward the steps that led to an escape from the ship.

Jan moved after him. "I know now! It was you who took the Chinese figure. You were there at Mrs. Pendleton's with your recorder and that flight bag. We were all talking to Eddie on the stairs and nobody was paying any attention to you. You saw a chance to get even with Eddie and Patrick. You put that brass jar in place of the image and covered it with the cloth. Then you must have popped the figure into your flight bag — and nobody even guessed."

The look on Neil's face was that of a person who had been living for some time in a make-believe world, and who had suddenly wakened to find himself faced with a terrible reality.

Patrick and Eddie were listening in astonishment and Jan went right on.

"All that about Eddie taking the image and hiding it in the ship was made up, wasn't it? It was you who put it there — so you could make things look bad for Eddie."

Neil waited for no more. He turned toward the steps and fled from the ship. At almost the same instant Patrick took off after him. Jan did not stay to see what sort of fight they would get into. She no longer cared. Neil and Patrick and Eddie could go ahead and work things out any way they liked. Nothing mattered except her own desperate reality.

Like Neil, she took to sudden flight, rushing off the boat and down the wharf toward shore. She did not so much as turn to look behind, but ran and ran through little streets where tourists walked in the sunlight and puddles were drying along the way. If people turned to stare, she paid no attention. She had to get to Gran's quickly. This whole thing had grown too big for her to handle. Gran had to be told, no matter what the result for Janice Pendleton might be. Only Gran could decide what to do about telling Miss Althea all that had happened.

The bookstore was empty of customers when she reached it, her grandmother was turning away from the telephone. The moment Jan saw her face she knew the worst had happened.

"I've just phoned for someone to help in the store, so I can leave early," Gran said. "Your great-grandmother called to say she's had a terrible shock. She happened to look in the place where the Chinese image was supposed to be—and it's not there. Janice dear, you must tell me the truth. Do you know where the china figure is?"

Jan was out of breath from running. She faced her grandmother, panting a little, and braced herself with her feet apart and her hands clasped behind her back.

"It's—it's at the bottom of the river!" she managed to gasp.

Gran reached for a chair and sat down. She pressed her fingertips to her forehead as though a headache had begun to thump in her temples.

"This is too much," she murmured. "I'm afraid it was a mistake to bring you here. We've grown very fond of you, Janice, but Mother and I are too old to face the problem of taking care of a child anymore. You've brought us so much more trouble than I would ever have dreamed was possible. This is the last straw."

It was clear what her grandmother meant. She could not stay in Mystic. She would have to go to Boston in the fall. Probably she would not even be allowed to keep her upstairs room for the remainder of her visit in Gran's house. And there was nothing she could say. Nothing at all. Because who was to tell for sure by now whose fault anything was? All that had happened was inter-twined. If Eddie and Patrick had made mistakes that led to trouble, so had she. It was entirely her fault that Neil Kent had been brought into this affair at all. The fact that no one was entirely to blame all by himself hardly helped matters at this stage, and it would not change Gran's feelings, or make easier the problem of explaining all this to Miss Althea.

"Do you want me to tell you what has happened?" she asked Gran a bit timidly.

A customer came in just then and Gran shook her head. "We'll go home soon," she said, "and you can tell Mother your story. If the Chinese image is gone, there isn't any way to soften the blow. She will have to hear the whole truth, whatever it is."

Jan sat in the pleasant reading room, with books on the shelves all around—and could not so much as look inside a book. There were no wonderful ideas chasing one an-other about in her mind any more. Her wits seemed to have turned to cotton wool. She could think of how awful everything was, but she could not think how to fix it. She did not even wonder what Patrick and Eddie were doing to Neil. Whatever it was, it would make every-thing worse and would land them all in that much more trouble. She could not bear to think about anything. She wished she could turn into a turnip and feel nothing. Perhaps this was how Miss Althea felt when everything was too much for her. But you could not be a vegetable by wishing it.

How much time passed before a woman arrived to help in the store and Gran was ready to go home, Jan was not sure. She was hardly aware of anything outside herself until Gran — no longer looking pink-cheeked and cheerful as she usually did — picked up her handbag and called to Jan to come along as she started for the door.

They walked together to the parking lot. Jan was still wearing her rain things, she noted in dull surprise. In the car she wriggled out of her coat and pulled off her boots. This gave her something to do on the way home, since she found it hard to sit quietly in the car.

"Home!" She wished she had not thought of the word. It made everything hurt all the more.

As they drove across the bridge and onto the road along the riverbank, Gran reached out and patted Jan lightly on the knee.

"Things do work out — somehow," she said. "This is hard to get through, but afterward you'll feel better."

How could she ever feel better? Jan thought. Not with the Chinese image gone and all the hurt and worry still to be dealt Miss Althea.

When they reached the house and went upstairs together, they found the old lady waiting for them in her favorite chair. Grandpa Marshall was with her and the little sailboat, *Happy Heart*, occupied the center of the table where Neil's tape recorder had rested a few days ago.

Surprisingly, Miss Althea looked far from sick or weak with shock. There was a touch of pink in her usually pale cheeks, and she had dressed herself in her favorite jade-green robe. Her white hair had been neatly combed and her eyes were bright. Here was no vegetable, certainly, but a person who was very much involved in living.

"Look what Thomas Marshall has made for me," she said, as Gran and Janice entered the room, and turned her pleased look upon the model.

Grandpa Marshall smiled delightedly as he rose to go, but Miss Althea stopped him.

"Wait, my old friend. I'd like you to stay while I find out what has happened. If I hadn't wanted to show you the Chinese image with its 'happy heart' message, I wouldn't have known it was gone."

Gran tried to open the matter gently. "Janice has something to tell us, Mother. Something unfortunate has occurred, and I'm afraid—"

Miss Althea tapped a slippered foot impatiently on the pale-gold rug. "What has happened to the figure, Janice? Have you taken it again?"

Jan shook her head and swallowed hard. She hated to talk about this before Patrick's grandfather, but there was no escape, and suddenly she knew where she must start her story.

"I didn't take it, though I know where it is," she said. "But first, I want to tell you about the jade Kwan Yin. No one was trying to steal it that day. Patrick was putting it back for his brother."

"Of course, of course," Miss Althea said impatiently. "I knew it was one or the other of them putting it back."

"But—you cried!" Jan said, puzzled. "You behaved as though something terrible had happened."

"It had," Miss Althea admitted. "I had just taken a close look at an old woman who had allowed herself to grow so far away from life that she had tried to buy her own peace of mind with a statue of jade. That was such a sad picture for me to look at, so of course I cried. I was ashamed of myself. But this doesn't tell me where the Chinese image has gone."

Clearly there was no use in trying to postpone telling

the whole story. Jan braced herself for the worst and blurted out the dreadful fact.

"I found out that it was gone and I tried to get it back. But I was too late. It's at the bottom of the river. Patrick threw it in the water from the deck of the whaling ship over at the Seaport."

Grandpa Marshall made a startled sound. Miss Althea sat very still, her eyelids fluttering lightly. Then she opened her eyes and looked straight at Jan with her wide green gaze.

"Good!" she said. "Now I shan't have the reproachful old thing around any longer telling me to be happy. I don't need him any more. I've made my choice. I know now that there's only one practical way to be happy in this life. No one owes us happiness, whatever age we are. We have to take care of that little matter ourselves. This means staying in the middle of life and caring about what happens to other people. I don't need that ugly, snarling old thing to tell me that!"

Grandpa Marshall clapped his hands together softly as if he applauded. Gran made a small, choked sound that was remarkably like a giggle, and she and Jan looked at each other in relief. For the moment they could forget their worst fears about upsetting Miss Althea. The old lady was fully alert and interested, and not at all upset.

It was possible now to tell the whole story from the beginning, and Jan did the best she could with all its complications. Once Gran asked a question to make a point clear, but Miss Althea said, "Do hush and let the child continue."

As Jan tried to reconstruct what had happened in the light of everything she knew, she realized that she no longer felt as critical and mistrustful of Patrick and

Eddie. Only Neil had been seriously at fault. What he had done was pretty awful and she could not think what the outcome would be. Especially if Eddie and Patrick gave him a thrashing.

She had reached the moment in her story when Patrick had dashed upstairs from the hold, with the Chinese image in his hands, to toss it overboard from the stern of the ship — when a clatter sounded nearby, as if several people were running up the outside stairs.

"Mrs. Pendleton!" someone called, and Jan recognized Patrick's voice.

"Go let them in!" Miss Althea commanded.

Jan jumped up and ran to the porch door. The three were there — Eddie, Patrick, and Neil. The two boys wore wet dungarees and Neil was without a shirt. All three looked excited. In his arms, well wrapped in a green-checked shirt, Neil held a bulky object.

Jan stared first at the three, then at the thing Neil carried. "Is — is it — ?" she began scarcely daring to believe.

"Well, tell them to come in!" Miss Althea cried. "What are you waiting for? I want to talk to those three. For once they're going to listen to me, old lady or not!"

It was Eddie who answered. He came through the door, looking a bit startled when he saw his grandfather. But he smiled broadly at Miss Althea, as Jan had never seen him smile before. "Sure, we'll listen, but the kids can't come in. They're soaking wet, and they'd ruin your rugs."

"Nonsense!" Miss Althea cried. "These rugs are a hundred years old or more, and they've seen worse. Besides, boys are more important than rugs. Bring them in!"

The two boys followed Eddie through the door. In her jade-green robe, Miss Althea sat like a queen awaiting her subjects, and they approached in sheepish silence, casting doubtful looks at Grandpa Marshall as they came. But silence was something Miss Althea would not have.

"Well—out with it! What have you three been up to? Not diving into that river to get my horrible old friend back, I hope!"

Patrick and Neil looked at each other in dismay, but it was not, Jan saw, a look of hostility. Though it seemed hardly possible, they seemed to be accepting each other, to a degree at least. Neil smiled self-consciously, looking not at all his old boastful self, and set down his burden beside Grandpa Marshall's sailboat. While everyone watched, he unwrapped the wet green shirt and in a moment Old Fang-Tooth was snarling at them, newly chipped chin and all.

Miss Althea glared back at the familiar face for a long moment. Then she sighed. "Why did you have to bring him home? Now I'll have to live with him again, and he will reproach me for the rest of my life. I don't see why my father had to set him watching me!"

Jan dropped to her knees beside the table and turned the figure over to show the place where the word "Rose" had been broken away. Her hands were clumsy because she was so excited. The idea had come back to her full force and she must find out for sure.

"I don't think your father meant for it to watch you, Miss Althea," she said. "Why don't you just smash it up and be done with it?"

Her great-grandmother considered the suggestion with obvious shock. "I couldn't possibly do that!"

Jan went to a table on which there was a silver bowl of

walnuts. She picked up the heavy old-fashioned nut-cracker as the handiest tool she could find and returned to the hassock.

"Then I'll smash it for you," she said.

Gran gasped and Patrick said, "Hey!"—but before anyone could stop her, Jan turned the figure on its side and began to chip away at the clay base where the message had been written.

The clay was old and brittle. The rest of the figure had been fired, but this layer of clay had not. Gillespie Osborn must have spread it across the base in order to have something to set his message in—a message no casual finder would figure out, but which he must have hoped would have meaning for his daughter. The trouble was that all his preaching about happiness, and his writing of articles about it, had thrown her off.

"He said to *find* something," Jan murmured, chipping until bits of dry clay scattered across the rug. "Something at the very *heart*. Something *happy*—something joyful."

"Give it to me, please," Miss Althea said. "Give it to me!"

Jan handed her the image and gave her the nutcracker as well. The old lady set the china figure on her knees and tapped more furiously at the clay base than Jan had done. The last big chunk of it loosened and with it came the thing that had been stuck to the clay—walled in, secretly hidden within the hollow image for all these years.

Miss Althea let the figure roll from her lap and held up the object on her palms, exclaiming in wonder. "It can't be—it can't be! Look, children. Look what my father sent me!"

A small green mound several inches high rested on her

palms. It was a mount of jade with trees and foliage carved into it as if they grew in the stone. There was a tiny waterfall and stream, and a little bridge. All around the mound were small houses and tiny Chinese men and women. Miss Althea turned the jade piece gently in her hands so they could all admire the lovely scenes a long-ago artist had known lay hidden in this lump of jade.

"My Joyful Mountain," Miss Althea murmured. "This was my favorite of all my father's collection. And it was the most precious. It was too large to take away in my handbag and I thought it had been lost. All these years I thought it had been lost!"

It was Neil's exclamation that broke the spell that lay upon them all. "That hunk of jade sure must be worth a lot of money!"

Miss Althea smiled. Gran almost giggled again, and Eddie and Patrick exchanged looks. Jan found herself regarding Neil rather sadly. He had so much to learn. He didn't know that true worth did not necessarily lie in the money value of an article. The worth of the jade mountain was far greater to Miss Althea than any amount of money could ever be.

"So my father wasn't preaching at me, after all," the old lady said, faintly amused now, though still marveling. "All the time the real happy heart was there behind Old Fang-Tooth's snarl, but I couldn't see what he really intended. It took a young great-granddaughter, all these years later, to find what the rest of us missed."

This was Jan's time of glory, and it was more satisfying than any make-believe because it was actually happening. For once she was the heroine of the moment.

Grandpa Marshall drew their attention from the jade mountain to put the next question. "How did you get the image back if it fell into the river?" he asked the boys.

They exchanged sheepish looks again, and it was Eddie who explained. "We were pretty sore at Neil when we found out his nutty plan to get Patrick and me in trouble. So when Pat ran down to the wharf, I went after him to help with anything he meant to do to Neil. But Neil wasn't trying to get away. Before we could catch him, he'd kicked off his shoes and run to the end of the wharf to dive into the river."

As Eddie's voice went on with the story, Jan could see exactly how it must have happened. The other two had realized what Neil meant to try, and they stood at the end of the wharf watching. Neil surfaced a few times and then went down again. He was a good swimmer and he had done a lot of scuba diving. Although this was different, he wasn't afraid under water.

The fourth time up he shouted that he had spotted the image. It was stuck in a mudbank and he couldn't get it loose. Then Patrick kicked off his shoes and dived in to help him. Between the two of them, they managed to loosen the heavy thing from the mud and bring it up. Eddie reached down to take it from them. After the two boys had climbed onto the wharf again, they all started for the place where Patrick had left his boat and had come across the river, their grudges forgotten in the common project of getting the image back to old Mrs. Pendleton.

"I guess we've all made a lot of mistakes," Eddie concluded ruefully. "By this time none of us can tell who's to blame for what."

This was the very thing she had decided, Jan thought.

"Nevertheless," Miss Althea said, "what Neil has done is very serious. The fact that he has been living in a spiteful, imaginary world doesn't excuse him for trying to harm others. What are we do do about you, Neil Kent?"

Neil, who had begun to look faintly cocky again, wilted, staring at the old lady in silence. Her eyes held his and he seemed unable to shift his gaze.

"What is the worst possible punishment you could receive?" Miss Althea asked him at last.

Neil proved his courage then. Looking her straight in the eye, he told her the truth. "To tell my father what I've done."

There was a long silence while Miss Althea looked questioningly from one to another about the room. Now Neil could shift his gaze. His eyes met Jan's and she gave him a halfhearted smile. Because—in a way—she understood Neil. Although she would never try to hurt anyone else, she too sometimes lived in a make-believe world and got it mixed up with reality.

"Well?" the old lady asked. "What do you all think?"

No one said a word until Patrick spoke up. "I guess he only meant it as a joke in the beginning, but it got away from him and it was too big to stop."

"It was a stupid joke," Neil admitted.

Eddie said slyly, "Maybe everyone needs a second chance. Maybe we could put him on parole, on probation."

Neil looked so ashamed that Jan felt sorry for him.

"Very well," Miss Althea said, "that is what we'll do. Do you understand me, Neil?"

He nodded miserably and she smiled at him more kindly. "I'd like to hear the interview you recorded sometime. Will you bring it over soon and play it for me?"

He brightened a little. "Sure," he said. "I'd like to do that."

Grandpa Marshall reached out and touched the sailboat lightly. "The charm is beginning to work," he said, and Jan knew he meant what Miss Althea was doing—

involving herself once more with other people, which was the only true way to a happy heart.

Everyone had relaxed a bit after so much high tension, and it seemed to Jan that this was a good moment to ask her own important question.

"Gran, do you think I can stay here?" she beseeched. "Do you think if I try hard not to be a bother, I can—"

Miss Althea broke in at once. "Who said there was any question about your staying? This is where you belong, isn't it? Aren't you happy in the room we've given you? Don't you want to stay?"

"Oh, I am, I am—I do, I do!" Jan cried. She looked at Gran and saw tears in her eyes, even though her grandmother was smiling and nodding.

With a gesture that carried all the warmth of her own loving heart, Jan flung her arms about Miss Althea and put her cheek against her great-grandmother's wrinkled one, holding her close.

"Don't smother me," Miss Althea said tartly, but she did not push her away.

Jan hugged her again and looked around the room. Neil had picked up the Joyful Mountain and was examining it curiously, probably still wondering about its money value. Patrick and Eddie were regarding each other intently and Jan knew the look was one of affection and trust.

Some time later, when the boys and Eddie and Grandpa Marshall had gone, when everything was quiet again, Jan sat on her bed in a room that was hers for as long as she needed it. She couldn't help hugging herself—the way she had hugged Miss Althea. There were a great many things to think about, and it would take a while to digest them all.

Nearby on her bed table she had placed the new friend Miss Althea had given her. Not Kwan Yin this time, but Old Fang-Tooth himself. He sat somewhat rockily on his straw mat, lacking a smooth base. Except for a chipped chin, he was otherwise unharmed. Jan grinned at him impudently. His expression no longer frightened her. Poor old thing—that was the only way he knew how to smile.

As for herself, she wasn't even homesick at the moment. Of course she missed her faraway family, but here she had a new family close at hand to whom she also belonged. And she had a new friend. Before he left, Patrick had asked, stammering a little, if she wanted to go for a ride in his boat sometime tomorrow. A dinghy with an outboard motor was scarcely the *Happy Heart,* but she had been glad to accept. She would dress properly for his boat this time, and not mind a little dirt.

Jan curled up on her bed and reached for the book that waited for her. It was possible to give herself once more to the story of Sara Crewe, the little princess. Sara was in much worse trouble than Jan Pendleton had ever been, and she could sympathize with her all the more because of her own recent difficulties.

She began to read and her surroundings faded. She was back in London in an attic room, and there was the kindhearted gentleman from India who could make a dream come true . . .

Jan's eyes were shining as she read and she did not know that Miss Althea opened her door softly and stood looking at her for a little while, her own eyes warm and loving. Then she went away, and the girl who was lost in the reading of a book went on turning page after page—right on to the magical end.

A WORD
FROM THE AUTHOR

I HOPE THAT many readers of this book will have the opportunity to visit Connecticut and see Mystic Seaport for themselves. I had read about it for a long time, and had seen photographs and paintings that have been made there. So when I decided to write an adult novel set in the long-ago days of clipper ships, I chose Mystic as the place to do a good deal of my research.

As soon as I saw Mystic Seaport I knew that this authentic, old-time village, which has been reconstructed on the bank of the Mystic River, would make a perfect place for a modern mystery story for young people. For several days I walked about the Seaport, visiting the museums and exhibits, learning how people used to live in the days when sailing was all-important to the New England coast. The rope walk — a place where rope used to be made — was an especially eerie place, with its long, tunnellike corridor and echoing interior. It was interesting to think of a story scene that could be set there, and the wheels of my imagination began to turn.

Perhaps the most interesting experience of all was my visit aboard the *Charles W. Morgan,* the last of the whaling ships. Here you can walk the decks and stand at the steering wheel. You can go below where the captain's cabin and the steerage area are all on view. It is possible to climb down still another ladder into the lower hold, which is very much as I've described it in my story. I knew at once that I must set a story scene aboard the *Morgan*. And so I did when I came to the writing of the book.

One thing, however, I must make clear because I know the questions that will come to me from readers if I do not. If you visit Mystic, you need not ask for Grandpa Marshall at the rope walk, or for Janice's Gran at the bookshop. Eddie Marshall will not be there to show you aboard the whaling ship, nor will Mr. Chilton be available at the museum. Though there is a marina upriver from the Seaport, it is not owned by the Marshalls, the family in my story. Nor are Eddie's difficulties based on those of any real person in Mystic. Any Pendletons, Marshalls, or Kents who happen to live in Mystic are not the families of my story.

Just as it is when a motion picture company goes into a real place to make a filmed story and sets its own actors to playing out the parts — so it is with a writer. With apologies to the real Mystic Seaport, I have set my own actors on the scene and for the time it will take you to read this book you can feel that they are really there moving through their roles in the story. But when you close the book, that is where they will stay, between its covers.

Having visited Mystic and written this book, I know that I am a richer person because of a unique opportunity to step back into the past and see how it really was while the history of our country was in the making. It has been fun to share this experience with my readers.